FAE'S HEART
FATED MATES OF THE FAE ROYALS, SUMMER COURT BOOK 4
HELEN WALTON

Helen Walton's fictional characters, locations, plot lines, places, events, and storylines are all the product of the author's imagination or are used fictitiously. Any resemblance to real persons, living or dead, is purely coincidental and is not intended by the author.

www.helenwaltonbooks.com

Walton House Publishing

CONTENTS

FOREWARD

A UTHOR NOTE
Choosing character names is not always easy, and there are times you pick them to mean something for the character and the story. I've included the pronunciation and meaning of the names, and if you're like me, and like to know and still pronounce the names the way you read them, then welcome to my club.

Niamh pronounced neeve meaning radiance.

Fintan pronounced fin-tan meaning white fire.

Eamon pronounced aim-on meaning keeper of riches.

Maeve pronounced may-veh meaning intoxicating.

Diarmuid pronounced deer-mid meaning without enemy.

Orlaith pronounced or-lah meaning golden princess.

Rian pronounced ree-an means little king.

Briana pronounced bree-a-nah meaning noble.

Aislinn pronounced ash-lin meaning a vision or dream.

Saoirse pronounced seer-sha meaning freedom.

Lorcan pronounced lor-can meaning silent or fierce.

Ciara pronounced kee-ra meaning dark.

Roisin pronounced row-sheen meaning little rose.

Donagh pronounced done-acka meaning brown-haired warrior.

Deirdre pronounced deer-dree meaning broken-hearted.

Malachi pronounced mal-lah-key means messenger of God.

Ailbhe pronounced all-bay meaning white.

Tadhg pronounced tie-guh meaning poet or philosopher.

Eabha pronounced ey-va meaning life.

For the warrior will battle
the flames for love.

PROLOGUE
RIAN 10 YEARS AGO

THE LUSH, OLIVE-GREEN VINES hanging from the atrium ceiling around the Spring Baile concealed my presence. I wasn't trying to hide, but luck meant the plants concealed me when my sister breached the locked Veil separating the Summer Court and Earth. The air hummed with power as Saoirse lifted her hand in a glimmering pink display. Her lips pursed in concentration. She peeked over her shoulder at the doorway. No one entered. Only Fae royals frequented this most sacred of places in the center of the palace unless there was a dire reason for its aid. Saoirse flicked back her long silvery blonde hair, turned to the lock, and opened the Veil. She stepped through and disappeared into the glowing mist.

Mere seconds later, the Fae King's shadow flitted across the doorway as he walked by the entrance to the atrium. As the eldest son and next in line to the throne, Father always seemed to want to teach me about our great powers over nature. I counted off inside my head until I reached one hundred before stepping out from behind the vines. The leaves reached toward me as though they wanted to embrace me, keep me by their side, and absorb my power. I brushed a soothing hand over the foliage, sending a pulse of my power into the stems. The vines burst into a display of pearlescent fluffy white flowers. The heady, perfumed scent of the blooms permeated the air. Beside me, the water in the spring gurgled as though delighted.

A lie.

The spring was diminishing little by little each year and no one in the family understood why. Now the change was becoming noticeable to the Fae outside the palace. The slower flow of water was affecting the Summer Court too. Let alone the fact if the spring stopped running, we'd lose our immortality.

I reached for the locked Veil. For too many years, the king had secured us inside the Summer Court. I hadn't witnessed the massacre the Trappers had wrought on the Fae living on Earth as Father had forced me, the next in line to the throne, to stay protected in the Summer Court. My grandparents hadn't escaped the destruction, though. The Trappers had caught them and burned them alive at the stake in a false attempt to steal our Fae powers. Many centuries had passed since we lost them and so many others, but we still suffered the pain of those times.

My power hummed in my palms, making them glow, and a jolt ran through my veins, building the surge until the lock clicked open and the Veil parted. I stepped inside the glimmering bronze-gold mist, letting the static current circle around me as I searched for the location Saoirse had journeyed to. *There*. A tangible thread of her power thrummed through the bronze-gold. I grasped the thread and followed the connection to Earth. The Veil parted for me like a welcoming curtain.

Stepping onto the soil of Earth always felt distinct, and today was no different. The ground was firmer here. Unyielding in its hardness. A tad like my heart at times.

Saoirse's form, draped in a pale pink dress, skipped along a large river of murky brown water. She looked out of place on the riverbank, but she was always most at home by water since her power commanded it.

I let out a long breath of despair. This filthy-looking water wouldn't be the source of our Spring of Life. Our water was clear, like fine crystal. My crown of thorns tightened around my head, as agitated as me. We needed to find the source of our spring so we could discover why the water was dwindling before we ceased to exist. Father was adamant that wouldn't happen, but I wasn't so sure.

Saoirse kneeled on the bank and shoved her hands into the water. A bird called a 'moo-co' alarm in the distance. The Horned Screamer sat in a tall Brazil nut tree, its dark gray and black feathers blending with the bark of the straight trunk. Its horn-like structure protruding from its crown reminded me of the unicorns back home. Saoirse whirled around, checking her surroundings, and sending water droplets everywhere.

Her power flared as she searched for a location that might be the cause of our spring's decline that was barely perceptible to anyone but us royals who were in constant contact with the spring. In an instant, she vanished back through the Veil and to the safety of the Summer Court. Her jumpiness was understandable after she witnessed our grandparents burned to death at the stake by the Trappers.

I had no such qualms in the face of danger. Father, Lorcan, and the King's guards had vanquished every Trapper on Earth. The threat from them was no longer. There were other dangers on Earth, but as immortals, we were hard to kill. Hard, not impossible.

The abundance of vibrant green trees, ranging from cocoa trees with their deep red pods to the monkey bush with its bright red and yellow flowers resembling brushes. Then to giant Mahogany trees famous for their redwood rustled as a flock of Oriole blackbirds took flight sounding more warning calls in their wake. Their bright yellow feathers were like specks of glowing gold in the sky. Black spider monkeys swung through the branches, their hands and tails gripping the banana trees and the climbing wooden Lianas vines hanging between the foliage in their haste to get away. They looked like their namesake. My power vibrated in readiness to call whatever element of nature to my aid. As a Fae prince, I possessed all the powers accessible to the Fae King, but to a lesser extent. The King would best me in a fight, but he was the King for a reason. To protect and serve our people. I'd learned a lot from Father and before him,

Grandfather, who'd been King before his unfortunate death, had groomed me to take over the title of Fae King one day if the unthinkable ever happened to my father.

At a glance, one would think the jungle was normal, but the absence of sound was a warning a predator stalked through the foliage. I searched to the left and right of me, detecting no movement. The hairs on my arms stood to attention. I spun, facing the forest instead of the river. Saoirse wouldn't be back. At least she was safe in the Summer Court.

My breathing came in shallow pants. Not because I was afraid, but so I didn't give away my position with too much sound. The beat of my heart would alert the predator, though, and the scent of my sweat in the sticky air would be a calling card. I should unlock the Veil, step back home, and be safe from this danger. Part of me recognized I should do that. The other part told me to stay. A sense something important was about to happen filled my body with anticipation.

A leaf swayed on a limb high above my head. My gaze snapped to scan the treetops. Shadows enveloped the thick jungle. The shadows were at home here among the variety of trees. They lived there in the depths of the foliage. I did not. A movement to my left caught my peripheral vision. *There*. A predator stalked me.

Jaguar.

The cat was as black as ebony silk. Her limbs were sleek for a killing machine. Luminous green eyes blazed at me from the depths of the shadows. The cat's black lids blinked in slow motion, making the entire jaguar disappear before its green orbs snapped back to life.

Time seemed to stop. Every nerve in my body yelled at me to go to the big cat. To embrace the creature as mine.

Mine.

The word pounded through me.

I tipped my head to the side. The cat copied me. The corners of my lips tugged as I fought a smile. I tilted my head the other way. The cat copied me again. This time, the smile came. The jaguar bared her teeth at me. I threw my head back and laughed.

A growl was my answer.

"Love," I called. The word echoed through the jungle. "Come down here and let me meet my mate."

The jaguar hissed. Turned her nose up and stalked the length of the branch to the Ironwood's trunk. She stretched up and clawed at the brown-gray bark.

"Aye, you are beautiful in this form. Come closer and show me."

She jumped down from the tree. Her sizeable paws landed on the solid earth with a soft thud. Inch by inch, she stalked closer to me, her tail twitching the entire time. Her whiskers too, as she scented the air.

"Dia, I never expected to find my fated mate on Earth." I crouched and held out a hand.

Her warm, damp nose met my palm. A deep purr vibrated in her body. I wanted to purr, too. For so long, I'd wanted a fated mate. The one meant for us and us alone. But being locked inside the Summer Court, the chances of finding the one destined for us were slim and growing slimmer by the days passing us by. My heart surged with power and the rightness of this moment. Of being in the presence of my fated mate.

She ducked her head and stepped closer. I ran my palm along the top of her head, sinking my fingers into her thick pelt.

"You're exquisite." I inhaled to stop myself from burying my face in her fur and scooping her up in my arms to hold her tight, and never let her go.

The jaguar stepped back. Her body quivered and contorted. Fur flashed and rolled as her body stretched, skin replaced the fur, and she stood before me as a woman. Long, licorice black hair hung down her body, over the curves of her breasts and brushing her dark nipples into hard peaks. My mouth watered to suck on them. To claim her as mine. My gaze traveled lower over the indent of her belly button, to the curls trying to hide the scent of arousal coming from between her legs.

"Who are you?" she asked, her voice soft, yet with a note of steel.

"Your mate." I bowed my head. "Rian O'Cleirigh Fae Prince of the Summer Court."

Her dark eyebrows rose, dragging my gaze to her face. I drank in her beauty. The sparkle of her green eyes, the fullness of her rosy cheeks, and the plump hue of her lips. How I longed to kiss them. All of her. Every inch.

"A Fae Prince!" Her hands covered her heart. The heart which was mine. As mine was now hers. "It's been many years since the Fae lived on Earth. The stories passed down over the years say you all died."

"No, not dead. Protected in the Summer Court."

Her hand shook as she reached out and touched my cheek with her fingertips, as though she wanted to make sure I was real.

"You can touch me whenever and however you like. I'm yours from this day forward."

Her fingers swept up into my hair, the caress growing firmer until she touched my crown.

"And I'm yours?"

I cupped her hand and held her palm against my face. "Aye."

"I sense that in my heart."

"As do I."

"Do you intend to claim me now?"

I grinned. "Aye."

SOPHIA

Dipping inside my mind, I found the link for our jaguar shifter telepathic bond and tugged the threads before speaking to my General, Laz, and my Lieutenant General, Ana.

"I've found my fated mate," I said. *"I'll be absent for our claiming ceremony."*

"What?" Laz asked.

"Congratulations," Ana said.

"Take care of the colony in my absence and if any poachers come near, then let me know."

"We'll be fine," Ana assured me.

"Who is he?" Laz asked.

"I'll talk to you both later."

I severed the connection and eyed the man before me.

The Fae Prince's smirk was charming. A testament to the confidence of being a royal. I should know, since I was royalty myself. The Queen of the Jungle.

"Seems presumptuous of you to claim me." I matched his smirk. "You don't even know my name."

He chuckled. "What is your name?"

"Sophia Moreno."

"Pretty like you."

I turned my hand under his and threaded my fingers with his. "Come. We have a special mating ceremony location."

"Interesting." He dropped into step with me. "What is involved with your ceremony?"

I batted my lashes at him. "Jaguar shifters are very secretive."

"I'm your fated mate. Shouldn't you tell me your customs?"

"Perhaps," I said. "What about your mating ceremony?"

"Ah, my mate would like my secrets first." He drew me closer to his body as we walked through the jungle.

The Amazon was home to me. Every lush green fern frond, every branch, and leaf familiar as we ventured into the thicker part of the jungle. Deeper and deeper, we walked away from the river. Rian scanned every direction with each step as though checking for any danger to him and me. What he didn't understand was I'd lived here all my life. If danger was around, the wildlife would alert me long before we'd see the threat.

"I suppose I do," I said after a moment.

"I won't need to tell you my secrets. When I place my mating mark on your chest, you'll have access to all my memories. You will see everything for yourself."

I stopped on a track that wouldn't be discernible for anyone but a local jaguar shifter.

"I'll see your memories?"

"Every single one of them." He placed his other hand on my chest over my heart. "Right here I'll place my mating mark. The process will hurt, but seeing my memories will hurt your head more. You'll slip into the Quiet to absorb them."

"What is this Quiet?" I asked, sensing the power humming in his palm, waiting to claim me.

He shrugged. "A place of rest for your body while your mind works."

I frowned. "I'm not sure what you're saying."

His indigo-rimmed blue eyes scanned the jungle again before settling on my face. "Humans call it a coma."

"I see." I narrowed my eyes. "And how long will I be in this coma, and out of action?"

"One can never be sure."

"I can't be out of action indefinitely. I'm the Queen of the Jungle," I burst out, thinking of all the jaguar shifters I helped stay hidden deep in the Amazon.

"Queen of the Jungle? I should have known my mate would be spectacular." He drew me into his embrace. "You're strong. Powerful. I doubt the Quiet would hold you for long."

"You doubt?" I pursed my lips.

"I have many years' worth of memories for you to absorb. It might take a while."

"How many years?"

"Five hundred and seventy."

I gasped. His lips landed on mine, swallowing my dismay at his age. At the sheer volume of memories someone so old would possess. The pressure of his lips was firm, claiming, and commanding. My body responded. I wrapped my arms around his neck as I drew him down to me, so I'd claim his mouth for mine, too. He opened his mouth so our tongues could tangle and tangle they did. A slide of damp heat as our mouths spoke more than words. Emotions were building in the kiss. How we both hungered for our fated mate. His palms warmed against my back, sending nerve-tingling sensations over my skin.

He kissed his way to the side of my mouth and cheek. "We need to hurry to your secret place before I claim you here and now."

I grinned and tugged his hand, so he fell into step with me again. "That's one way to shut me up."

Rian laughed. "My mate has an attitude."

"You don't know what you've gotten yourself into."

"I can't wait, Sophia."

I stopped at a thick wall of vines. Hidden beneath them was the entrance to our jaguar shifter mating cave. The place we came to when we found our mates because we needed a safe place to give into our carnal desires. Once a jaguar found their mate, they'd have sex for a week straight, not even stopping to eat. Rian didn't know what he was in for, but his arrogance told me he'd take it and then some.

"Are we here?" He squinted around the jungle.

"Almost. Before we step inside, promise me you won't mark me with your Fae mating mark until I've finished my jaguar claim."

His lips twitched. "My little jaguar queen is bossing me around already?"

"Promise."

He brushed his hands down my arms and cupped my hands in his. "I've waited many years for you, so I'll promise you anything to have you."

"Good," I said.

I extracted my hands from his and brushed the vines aside.

The cave entrance was dim. Rian peered through the vines, waiting for me to lead the way. I nodded my head in the universal gesture for 'come on' and walked into the cool entrance. The air inside the tunnel was damp with moisture, but the further we walked along the thick tunnel walls, the lighter the air became until we stepped into the cave. Rian sucked in a startled breath. I grinned, since that was the reaction I'd hoped for.

A soft light streamed inside the cave through a small opening and lit up the rocks. The colors of the rainbow shifted up the walls from buttery yellow to muted orange, burgundy red, teal green, indigo blue, and plum purple. A sense of magic caressed me. The cave was a sacred place for jaguar shifters made from ancient and mysterious rocks. Inside this cave, our jaguar settled into a pussycat. Now, mine purred.

Rian's gaze swung to me. "Did you just purr?"

"You've seen nothing yet." I slid my hands to his waist and caressed the tight muscles of his abdomen.

"Sophia." He sighed my name like a caress.

I lay my finger over his lips. "Shh. We'll talk later. For now, my jaguar side is clamoring to claim her mate."

He nipped my finger with his teeth.

I hadn't expected that from a Fae. A startled laugh escaped my lips. I slid my hand to his neck.

"I'm going to bite you here."

"Bite me all you like." He gave me a salacious grin.

"Oh, I will," I said. "Rian, I hope you've got stamina."

"Mate." He hauled me against his body and into his straining erection. "You don't need to worry about my endurance."

I ripped his shirt from his body with a swipe of my half-shifted claws. Since I was already naked, it brought us skin to skin, eliciting a tremble of need through us both. Rian shoved his hand between my thighs with no preamble to find me slick with need already. He dragged the moisture to my clit and circled the hard nub until my hips rocked against his palm.

"I can't wait to make you purr from an orgasm."

I snickered. "Who says I will?"

"I'll make sure of it."

He thrust two fingers into my slick heat, and suddenly vines were pulling at my legs. The vines circled my ankles and dragged me to the ground. Rian followed me as a layer of white flowers burst beneath my back and overhead the ceiling of the cave glittered with bright lights, like stars.

"Rian?"

"Hmm," he murmured as he nuzzled my neck. "'Tis just my powers celebrating finding you."

"It's beautiful."

"Thank you, my love."

"Love?"

"Aye. I'll love you forever. You're my heart. My everything."

He kissed me, claiming my lips as his fingers rocked inside me, building the tension in my body so hard and fast I scratched his back with half-shifted claws. It should have hurt him, but he kept kissing me, kept pleasuring me until my legs quivered as the tension tightened. My blood roared through my ears until I exploded in an orgasm that made me hold on to his body so I wouldn't float away on the bliss.

As he predicted, a purr vibrated in my chest.

"There's the sound I wanted to hear." He grinned in satisfaction. "I can't wait to experience your purr while I bury my cock deep inside you."

"Do it," I goaded.

He hauled my back off the ground, dragged me to his chest, and sat me on his lap. "Like this. I want to see your beautiful face as you come on me."

"And I was worried you wouldn't last our jaguar shifter's weeklong sex marathon."

His right eyebrow rose. "A week in here, with you, having sex?"

"Yes. Are you up for it?"

"More than up for it. But I'll need food."

He thrust up into me, impaling me with his cock and grinding my clit on his pelvis. My nipples rubbed against his smooth chest, sending a tingling ripple of arousal down to my core. His lips claimed mine in a scorching kiss, then roamed down my neck to suck on the tender flesh in the hollow of my shoulder.

"I can hunt for you," I half moaned, rocking my hips.

He met me stroke for stroke as he said, "I don't eat meat."

"Plenty of water apple trees near here." I gasped as each stroke brought the tension in my body tighter.

"Talk later," he growled.

"Much later," I agreed and buried my teeth in his neck, claiming him as my mate for all time.

CHAPTER ONE
SOPHIA
PRESENT DAY

T HE ENORMOUS BLACK WOLF chased me through the Australian forest in my jaguar form. He'd never catch me if I didn't want him to, but this had gone on far too long. I gave myself distance from the township of Crystal Creek before halting on the opposite side of the lake. At least here, out in the wilds of the forest, no one would overhear our conversation.

"Rian."

I reached for my mate through our telepathic bond. Jaguar shifters possessed the extraordinary power to talk mind to mind with our kind, and once we claimed our mates, we also formed those bonds.

"Aye, my love?" came his immediate response.

No matter where or what Rian was doing as a Fae prince and next in line to the Summer Court throne, he always answered me. Our lives since we'd claimed each other hadn't been ideal, but we both held the hope that one day soon, we'd unite the two kingdoms of Earth and the Summer Court with the Fae ruling both. For too long, the Fae had left Earth. And for too long, the humans had lost the powerful magic they possessed, making Earth a more uninhabitable place. The weather changed and became more volatile. Forests diminished without constant support. Lakes and rivers had dried up in some countries. Fires burned out of control in others. Although close to eighty years old, I wasn't old enough to remember those days, but my parents did. They'd passed their wisdom on to me, their only child, and their one hope I'd protect the jaguar species from extinction. Once we reached the age of twenty-five, our bodies never changed, and our immortality kept us young looking.

Now the Fae and the jaguars were heading the same way. The Fae's Spring Baile had depleted so much, it might stop. If what Rian said was true, then the Fae would lose their immortality, and they'd die like humans. I wasn't sure how that would impact us jaguar shifters.

I'd do anything to save my mate, as he would me.

"Your sister's mate has chased me through the forest."

"Which one?"

"Briana's mate. The big black alpha wolf," I spoke into his mind with such ease like we were two halves of one whole. *"It's time I talked to them."*

"I'll be there as soon as I can slip away."

"It's all right. I can handle myself."

Rian's chuckle vibrated inside my skull.

"I'm well aware you can."

I smirked. Which would appear like I was showing the wolf my teeth. A woman burst through the bushes and skidded to a stop next to the black beast. He accepted her presence without even sparing her a glance. His stare was for me. As the alpha of the wolf pack, he had every right to stare me down for being in his territory.

"Easy, you two," she said, waving her glowing hands. Vines grew from the ground with her power to slither under her control. "Don't make me tie you both up."

If a jaguar could laugh, then I would have. She was so like her brother. The wolf beside her shifted, and she shoved a pair of jeans toward him. He yanked them on while never taking his gaze off me.

"Which one of my brothers are you mated to?"

I cocked my head. *How did she know I'd mated with one of her brothers?* My whiskers itched with the vibrations in the air from her power. Letting go of my jaguar form, I shifted into a woman with ease. We were the same. A cat and a woman combined. I was at home in either form. Although now I possessed a Fae mate, I much preferred being a woman. I wished Rian was by my side for this meeting, but I understood how difficult it was for him to travel to Earth. How his father had locked them in the Summer Court after the Trappers slaughtered their numbers. Escaping to Earth wasn't easy.

But still....

I wished my mate was with me.

"Rian," I said, placing my hands on my hips. Nudity didn't bother shifters when we lived in the wilds of the Amazon jungle, and I assumed the wolves of Australia would feel the same.

Briana's eyes widened in shock. "Rian?" she spluttered.

"Yes, is that so hard to believe?"

"I thought for certain you'd be Lorcan's mate." She scoffed. "Rian's always been so... dedicated to Father's ways."

I shrugged. "We can't stop fate."

She swallowed hard. "You're his fated mate?"

She appeared sad. I didn't know why she'd be sad he possessed a fated mate.

"Yes."

"How long?"

"Ten years."

A gasp crossed with a sob burst free from her mouth.

Her mate hugged her. He let her bury her face in his chest while he rubbed soothing circles on her back. Envy clawed at my skin that my mate wasn't with me doing the same thing. She lifted her face and pushed out of his arms.

"Why didn't he tell me?"

"I'm sorry, Briana. You'd have to ask Rian."

"You know my name?" she asked, then tapped the side of her head. "Of course you do. You've seen his memories."

I laughed. She was cute in an annoying younger sister's way. I'd witnessed their interactions in Rian's memories. His other sisters were the same, although they all exhibited unique personalities and powers. His only brother, though, was a handful.

"I have a small cave close to here where I have clothes and tea. If you'd like to accompany me there, then we can talk more."

"Aye, I'd like that," Briana said. "Sledge, what do you think?"

"Yeah. I sure don't want to talk to your brother's mate while she's naked. I know how possessive fated mates are."

"Says the wolf shifter, who's happy to get naked." Briana rolled her eyes in a teasing way. "Lead the way."

"This way." I nodded my head to the west and walked in that direction.

Since I was the only one who lived here, the undergrowth was denser. The forest was wilder and more untamed than where the wolf shifter town was located. They controlled a large settlement. It gave me hope for our jaguars back home in the Amazon jungle that one day we'd have more plentiful numbers than they did. Hope, too, that perhaps there were more jaguar shifters around the world since Australia didn't have wolves in its ecosystem. Maybe after everything that occurred here on Earth, supernatural creatures had hidden even from each other.

It was an exciting thought.

My feet made soft patters on the soil and crunched the leaves wafting the eucalyptus odor around us. I'd never get used to it. I much preferred the scents of the Amazon jungle. Rian would take me back soon. From time to time, he'd brought me here to find out if his sister Saoirse was safe. She'd left the Summer Court when she'd found her fated mate in a wolf shifter by accident and had given birth to his baby. Briana kept visiting Saoirse too, and that's how she discovered her fated wolf mate, Sledge. It seemed like all the Fae royals were finding their fated mates on Earth. Funny, since the king meant to keep them locked in the Summer Court. Ridiculous, too. The Fae King imposed such a preposterous rule.

"Here we are," I said, pausing at a rock face holding the entrance to the cave.

"After you," Sledge said.

He didn't trust me. I wouldn't either if I was in my territory and a stranger claimed to be mated to a relative, and the relative hadn't told me. Of course, I'd think something was wrong. I padded into the cave. It was nowhere near as spectacular as the ceremonial cave back home, but this cavern was my little secure house right now. I shuffled over to a pile of folded clothes and put on a pair of shorts and a tank top, before lighting a small fire and placing the kettle over the flames.

"Please, have a seat."

There were only a few boulders to sit on, but Sledge and Briana sat and scrutinized me while I made mugs of tea in metal cups. I possessed nothing fancy here, but I'd owned nothing fancy all my life, not like the images I witnessed in Rian's mind of his palace. I didn't want to go there because I was too uncultured for a prince even though I was the Queen of the Jungle.

"So, um, I guess you want to know what I'm doing here?" I asked as I handed them their mugs.

"Yes." Sledge took the mug but didn't drink from it.

"Well, Rian's brought me here a few times to check on Saoirse. He worries about her being on Earth."

"We all do," Briana said. "It's how I ended up here."

"I overheard her when she was in labor as you made your way through the forest that night. I observed you both, but then you disappeared through the gap in the bushes, and I couldn't hear anything. My jaguar didn't like the magic coming from the bushes and wouldn't go inside. So, I circled the entire area, but I couldn't figure out the magic, so I sat up in a tree and waited." I glanced at Sledge. "I watched you and Saoirse's mate, Arrow, come through the forest and disappeared inside the bushes. Then you all came out with the baby."

"Why didn't you show yourself then?" Sledge asked.

"Rian didn't think it was the right time. Besides, you two had a big fight and—"

"You overheard us?" Briana asked.

"Yes, and you had every right to be angry with Sledge." I shot him a filthy glare. "No shifter should ever put their teeth marks on another after they've claimed a mate."

Sledge held up a placating hand. "Easy there, we've worked out I was an ass, and Briana's forgiven me."

I scoffed. "Did you make him grovel?"

Briana laughed. "My, you're feisty. I can't believe you're Rian's mate. He's always been so collected." She laughed again.

"Opposites attract, babe," Sledge said.

"Clearly." She rolled her eyes at her mate again.

"What were you doing by the waterfall today?" Sledge asked.

"Is that what's inside the magic barrier?"

"Aye," Briana said.

"Huh." I plonked down on a boulder and sipped my tea. "Not what I was expecting, but it makes sense Rian would want to know more about this. You sense a connection to the place. Is the waterfall connected to your Spring of Life?"

"Sorry to say, no." Briana sighed. "There's something there though, otherwise why would someone put a barrier around it?"

"You'd have to ask a priestess or witch. They're the only ones who can discern the different types of magic."

Briana shot Sledge a glance.

"I've called Pepper. She said she'd come when she's available, which, knowing her, might be anytime this year," he said.

"Who's Pepper?"

"A witch I know." Sledge sipped his mug of tea. "What's in this?"

"Tea, honey, and a dash of wild boar's blood, but don't worry Briana, I only put the blood in ours."

She smiled while Sledge threw back the rest of his mug like he was dying of thirst.

"When is Rian coming back to see you?"

CHAPTER TWO
RIAN

Every inch of my being itched with the need to go to my mate. A crawling sensation of beetles ran over my skin. A burning sensation of my blood pounding through my veins, and a buzzing pressure inside my skull. The feelings had grown worse over the years we couldn't be together every day. Now, when she'd spoken inside my mind, they'd intensified to the blazing heat of the sun.

"Rian, did you listen to what I said?" Father asked as he sat across from me in the drawing room, seated in the high-backed wing chair.

"Aye, Father." I forced myself to relax and appear like I possessed all the time in the realm to sit in this room and talk with him and my brother.

Lorcan leaned against the ornate fireplace that hadn't held a fire since the Trapper's destruction. His fingers flickered with bright green-blue flames though, a testament to the power inside him. The one that had helped Father put an end to every single Trapper while he had forced me to stay protected in the Summer Court.

I'd wanted to avenge the wrong doings against our family and people too. They had forced the pressure as next in line to the Fae throne on my head from before I could remember. I matched Father's look. Perhaps we were the same in many ways. He would have experienced this same pressure too when he was the prince. Now I understood his reaction to keeping us safe.

"I heard you, Father. I've heard you for many centuries, but if Saoirse found her fated mate outside of the Summer Court, then there is a likelihood other Fae will too."

His lips thinned into a tight line as the crown of thorns writhed around his head, sending his pale blond hair into disarray.

"I understand you all want a fated mate. Dia, I wanted one too and the thought of choosing a woman didn't sit well with me, but I would have performed my duty. I'd intended to choose a woman on my two hundredth birthday."

"Yet fate had other ideas. Don't keep us prisoners any longer."

His head reeled back as though the word 'prisoner' struck him across the cheek.

"I never intended to imprison the Fae."

"We know, Father." I leaned forward. "But here we are. Our people are restless here. They want the choice to return to Earth."

"I'm uncertain." He shook his head. "It's been too long. Humans might have forgotten us. Their lives are short. We'd be a story they whispered to each other in the dark of the night."

"How would you know?" Lorcan asked, his flames flickered up to his wrist now.

"Hypothesis." Father's gaze snapped to Lorcan.

A tense undercurrent of power erupted in the air as my brother and my father gave each other a loaded look speaking more than words.

"We need to do something," I butted into their silent conversation. "The spring is still declining. If the water stops flowing..."

"I'm well aware we'd become mortal if the spring ceased to flow." Father snapped his steely gaze back to me. "Ciara is searching through the books in the library."

Lorcan snorted. Our sister Ciara was smart and dedicated to finding the cure to our springs problem, but I doubted as much as Lorcan that we would find the answer in a book. I didn't bother saying this to Father though. I'd said this enough and yet he persisted the answer was here in the Fae Kingdom.

"Very well, I shall go help her." I stood from the plush chair.

"Aye, I'll help too," Lorcan said, and joined my side.

Father stood and gave us a curt nod, then strode from the room without a backward glance. Lorcan quietly closed the door behind him.

"We'll get him to see reason soon," Lorcan said.

"Soon may not be soon enough." I grimaced and reached for the mating mark on my neck.

"Will you ever tell me about your mark?" Lorcan nodded at my neck.

"Little brother." I cupped his shoulder. "More than anything I want to, but it's not the time."

"You can't keep your mate a secret forever."

"What makes you say I have a mate?"

He coughed. "It's easy to tell when you've enjoyed sex. Saoirse and I observed your change, but we didn't think you finding your mate was the reason. Not until she found hers did I put the connection together."

"You must miss Saoirse. You two were so close."

"Quick change of subject, brother. Aye, I miss her, and Father has his spy watching me, so it's been impossible to sneak away and visit her."

"I haven't visited her either. Only Briana has visited her location on Earth."

"Aye, and a good thing too she was there for the birth of Saoirse's baby boy. Now he'll possess Fae powers and wolf shifter abilities."

"An interesting combination," I said, wondering what my child with my jaguar shifter mate would produce if we ever enjoyed the chance to procreate.

"There are lots of combinations on Earth. There used to be a lot here too."

"Aye, I remember. Our two worlds were always meant to be combined. This separation is destroying them both, but Father doesn't care about Earth any longer."

"He will once he realizes your mate lives on Earth too."

"You are not to tell him." I glared.

"But—"

"No. She is... never mind... I must go to her now." I sent a surge of power into my palm and reached for the locked Veil. A swirling display of colors shimmered in the air as the lock gave way under my power.

"Rian, wait, how did you unlock the Veil here and not at the spring where our connection is strongest?"

"We possess the power of the royals we can do anything we wish with it. Father's power might be greater, but we can breach his lock anywhere." I stepped into the Veil leaving my brother to comprehend my words. He was smart, he'd figure it out.

We were all smart. That's why this challenge was so infuriating. We should be able to figure out the problem with our spring.

I exited the Veil on Earth to a soft breeze blowing through the forest I now stood in. The silvery-green leaves glinted in the sunlight streaming through the branches. A bird called, sounding like it laughed. The Australian Kookaburra. I'd learned the name while researching this place Saoirse now lived with her mate. The library in the Summer Court was good for some things. There was a magical connection between our library and the libraries on Earth so we could access the humans' books without ever leaving the Summer Court. A nifty trick our most ancient of Fae, the librarian Eabha, weaved with her power. Even she didn't know the origin of our Spring of Life which, considering her age, was a testament to how old the Fae were.

To my left sat the entrance to my mate's cave. I stepped inside and caught the rumble of a man's voice. Unease skittered through my powers making my hands glow. If he dared to hurt my mate, I'd tear his heart out of his chest. I inched along the wall keeping to the side and staying as hidden as possible using my powers to create a rock face that moved with me. Closer I stepped, one tiny pace at a time. My mate spoke. At least she was safe. A fraction of my unease lifted. As I neared the entrance to the cave, a woman's voice echoed in the interior.

Briana. What was my sister doing here?

"Rian," came my mate's amused voice inside my head. *"If I can scent you, I'm sure the wolf shifter can too. Just reveal yourself."*

"Wolf shifter? Why is he here with my sister?"

Sophia's laughter echoed inside the cavern and in my head.

"Rian is here now," she said.

Dia, my mate was so infuriating sometimes. She should have at least let me understand what I was walking into before outing my presence.

"Where?" Briana spun.

"Over by the wall," the man said.

I dropped the power holding the protective shield of rock before me. Briana grinned at me, but I stalked toward my mate and stepped in front of her.

"What are you doing here? And who are you?" I pointed my finger at the man.

Briana's smile grew. "This is Sledge, my mate."

My eyes widened then I narrowed them. "Your mate? Why didn't you tell me you mated?"

"I might ask you the same thing."

I folded my arms over my chest. "That's none of your business. What I and my mate agreed to tell people is between us."

"You're such an arrogant know-it-all," Briana said, standing and poking me in the chest.

My power snapped out to wrap her hand in a vine. Her power responded with a bright green flare and her own set of vines twirled with mine like two living snakes of leaves vying to win.

"Wow," Sledge said. "I didn't expect hundreds-of-years-old Fae to be so childish."

"Right?" Sophia said stepping from behind me.

Briana and I glanced at each other and snickered. Our vines vanished, and we hugged in a quick embrace.

"I suppose we should all talk," I said.

"I think we should involve Saoirse and Arrow too," Briana said.

"Aye, this involves them too."

"We'll head to their cabin now. Arrow's place is out of the town so no one will see you two," Sledge said. "I'd rather not have to explain another Fae in our wolf shifter town and a cat shifter."

"Jaguar." Sophia sniffed indignantly.

"All right," I agreed because I wanted to see for myself Saoirse and her baby were safe here. "We'll track you in a short while after I talk to my mate."

Sledge smirked like he grasped talk wasn't what I meant as he led Briana out of the cave. Alone with my mate, I turned toward her.

CHAPTER THREE

SOPHIA

I CROOKED MY FINGER at Rian. He was on me in an instant, devouring my lips with his as he yanked my hips against his building hardness. I sagged in his embrace, so happy to be back in my mate's arms. In his presence and being held by him. Worshipped by him because that was what he did. He adored every part of me, even the stubborn side and the feisty side.

His lips trailed from my mouth to my neck. "We should talk."

"Mmm hmm," I mumbled as his lips met the sensitive junction of my neck and shoulder.

His teeth scraped over my skin making my pulse jump.

"You shouldn't have let another man in here."

I dug my fingers into his shiny hair, holding his head still so he'd keep his mouth against my neck. "He's mated to your sister."

"I still didn't like it."

"Yeah, well, I don't like you in the Summer Court pretending you're not mated while your father is trying to set you up with women." I yanked his head away from my neck.

His indigo-rimmed blue eyes blazed at me. "I've ignored every single one of his demands."

"So you should." I huffed.

"We can't go on like this." He sighed. "Come back to the Summer Court with me."

"Remain here on Earth with me."

"If only..."

"Shut up and kiss me," I said. "I need you. It's been too long."

"Aye, my love, my heart, my everything."

His lips teased the edges of mine in a fluttery kiss so light it was barely there. One of those kisses that let me know he loved me and would do anything for me if I meant what I'd said when I said stay here on Earth with me. I didn't want that for Rian or us. We both held responsibilities to our races. Ones that took precedence over our mate status. But it'd be perfect if the Veil between our two worlds was unlocked, and he could come to me and I to him without restrictions. Those thoughts were for another time though. Right now, I wanted to feel only his body against mine as we spoke our special language of love.

I swiped my tongue over the seam of his lips. He opened as I knew he would. Our tongues tangled in a dance of desire and lust. His hands roamed my body as though he couldn't get enough of touching me. I did the same to him for I couldn't stop touching him. His firm back, tight buttocks, and around to the front where his erection strained against his pants. He rocked his hips into my touch and released my mouth long enough to tug my tank top over my head. He threw the garment aside then took my mouth in a ravenous kiss as his hands cupped the fullness of my breasts. I moaned into his mouth seeking more than a soft caress. He obliged by tweaking my nipples between his thumbs and forefingers.

My legs turned to jelly as desire shot straight to my core. Each tug made my stomach muscles tighten along with the growing ache between my legs to have my mate inside me. A tiny groan mixed with a snarl escaped my mouth. Rian swallowed the noise as his lips smiled against mine.

"I love the sounds you make," he whispered, breaking the kiss to nuzzle my neck once again.

"Stop teasing." I gasped as he bit my neck.

A flood of moisture coated my shorts. I stopped groping him to relieve myself of the restricting material. I wanted my mate to have access to all of me. Now. Rian's teeth didn't move as he held me in place, kicked my legs apart, and sought the slick junction between my legs. I bucked as his finger slid inside me with ease. He worked along the bundle of nerves inside my channel until I panted for breath and clutched at his arm.

He lifted his head. "Always so eager for me."

I pushed him back and tugged at his pants, not caring he still had on his shirt. What I needed was straining to be released from below. The rest of his clothes would come off later. Much later when he'd relieved this desire inside me that was burning me up from the inside out.

"Pants, now, Rian."

"My bossy little queen."

He wrenched my hands away and opened his pants. His long, thick cock sprang free. I sank to my knees eager to taste him. The second my mouth closed around him, a deep guttural groan rumbled from his chest. I loved the noises he made as much as he loved the ones I made and only we could make each other feel this way. I licked his cock from the base to the head and gazed up at Rian in reverence. The things my mate did that were all for me I wanted to return to him.

His hands cupped my face for a minute as he stared at me licking him until the point his eyes darkened with desire. His palms coated with his power in a way that made each touch on my skin alive with electricity. He wrenched my mouth off him, hauled me to my feet, and backed me into the wall. I wrapped my legs around his waist and hung on to him as he impaled me with his hard cock. Behind me, the wall burst into a soft cushion of vines as he thrust deep inside me. His hand cupped my head for protection, but I didn't need it. I was strong as a jaguar shifter. I clenched my thighs around his waist and tightened my muscles on his cock to remind him how strong I was.

He let go of my head and pushed me into the wall harder. Thrust into me more urgently until the only sounds in the cave were our ragged breaths and the slap of flesh on flesh. Until the tension inside me burst in a torrent of contracting waves in an orgasm leaving me gasping for breath. Rian held himself still and deep while the high kept me soaring in the place of bliss only my mate would take me.

"My love," he ground out, "you need to come for me again."

I cupped his face. "Make me."

He smirked. "Oh, I will."

Rian unhooked my legs from his waist and dropped them to the floor. Now I felt even fuller, and the instant buzz of arousal surged from the sensation. He stripped his shirt while keeping my hips pinned to the wall with his. The expanse of his well-muscled shoulders and chest was bare to my ravenous gaze. I soaked in the masculine beauty of my mate. My heart fluttered inside my chest that he was all mine. Forever.

He cupped my hands in his and pinned them over my head before lowering his mouth to a nipple. Rian sucked the hard peak into his hot mouth and rolled his hips in a circle.

"Oh, Rian." I moaned again and again as each circle of his hips ground against my clit and rolled his cock against my inner walls.

Pinned and helpless he kept up the ecstasy until every limb in my body shook. Every muscle tightened. Every nerve sparked with electricity to the point of a pleasure type pain I couldn't take any longer. He released my nipple from the ceaseless torment of his tongue and teeth to whisper in my ear.

"Come for me, mate."

The command was instantaneous. My body exploded taking Rian's along for the glorious ride. Higher and higher we soared into the very heavens, if they existed, as our bodies pulsed and contracted in time with the others. Two halves of one whole. I experienced this whenever I was with him and whenever we were apart, I suffered the tear in my heart.

Rian lowered my arms to his neck. I hugged him tight to me never wanting to let him go as it was all I ever seemed to do. He embraced my back, drawing me off the vines and wall into his warm embrace. For a long time, we stood there in the comfort of each other's arms until we both comprehended we couldn't stay locked together forever.

"I love you, no matter what," he said.

CHAPTER FOUR
RIAN

MY NAME MEANT 'LITTLE king', but when I was beside Sophia, I always felt minuscule. Her strength was so large, she would bring the entire world to its knees if she so desired. She could rule Earth if there was a way to make her their ruler, but Earth was in chaos. Humans were even more so. It'd never been like this when the Fae ruled Earth as one of their realms.

Father locking the Veil had further reaching consequences than any of us realized inside the Summer Court.

We dressed in silence, both of us knowing words were pointless right now as we basked in the afterglow of our lovemaking. I loved her so much. If I could allow myself the freedom to only think of her, then I would. I understood she felt the same way, but our sacrifices were wearing on us and creating a tension between us that shouldn't be there with fated mates.

I clasped her hand in mine and let her lead the way through the forest to Saoirse's new home. Since she possessed the tracking skills of a jaguar, she would follow the scent of Briana and Sledge with ease. The trek was a long walk through the thick bush. Branches reached for us as though trying to halt our approach the closer we walked to the town.

"There's a magical barrier around the town," Sophia said. "I can sense it."

"I love your powers."

"It would help if I could discern the type of magic."

"You don't give yourself enough credit." I slipped my arm around her waist and drew her side into my body.

She snuggled her head into the crook of my arm as our footsteps brought us out of the forest and in front of a cabin. They'd made the timber walls of logs from the forest, making it a part of its surroundings. As we crossed the small patch of dirt by the parked trucks outside the cabin, the front door flew open. Saoirse stood in the doorframe her pretty pink dress reminiscent of the ones she wore in the Summer Court, but she hadn't been back there for over a year. A smile broke out over her face the instant her gaze landed on me, and she ran down the steps and threw her arms around me and Sophia. I hugged her back while Sophia glared on awkwardly trying not to squirm out of the forced embrace.

"It's good to see you, Saoirse." I squeezed her hard then let go, hoping she'd take the hint.

She stepped back with a huge smile on her face.

"This is Sophia, my mate."

"So nice to meet you," Saoirse said. "Come inside and meet my mate and your nephew."

"I'm glad the pregnancy and birth went well for you."

"Me too." She ducked her head but not before I caught the glimpse of fear in her eyes. She'd been scared and we should have all been here for her.

"I should have come sooner."

"Perhaps." Her smile dropped. "I doubt it would have changed anything with Father."

"He's gradually coming around."

She scoffed and made her way back up the stairs. We followed her into the cabin and the large seating area holding a deep blue sofa. On it sat Briana, Sledge, and another man I assumed was her mate since he was holding a baby.

"Arrow, this is my brother, Rian and his mate, Sophia." Saoirse drew us over to Arrow. "Rian, Sophia, this is Arrow and our baby Ailbhe."

Arrow rose and held out his hand. I clasped his wrist in the greeting of olden times. He clasped mine and stared into my eyes with his golden gaze.

"If you intend on hurting Saoirse or Ailbhe, then I'll rip your throats out right here and now," Arrow said.

Beside me, Sophia growled. I sensed her urge to change into her jaguar form, so I placed a calming palm on her stomach to hold her back if she lunged at my sister's mate.

"I would never hurt my sister or her offspring."

"Good." Arrow nodded. "What about your mate?"

"Sophia?"

I peeked her way. Her eyes shone a luminous green. Her jaguar form was so close to the surface, she was struggling to contain the energy of the beast. I stepped in front of her, so she only had me to focus on and not the other predators in the room. Off to the side, the furniture creaked as the others stood, no doubt ready to jump in if we needed them. My mate needed to calm her feistiness before this situation got out of hand.

"My love," I said soothingly, "my heart, there's no threat to me here. You don't need to protect me."

Her nose twitched as though the jaguar's whiskers were on her face and my words vibrated them. Her gems of eyes snapped to mine. A claw-tipped hand traced the contours of my jaw.

"These are family members. They mean me no harm."

She blinked, her eyes losing a part of the luminous glow signaling her jaguar form. The tension in her body eased, and her lips loosened so her teeth weren't showing.

"Apologies," I said, facing everyone. "Sophia is very protective of me."

She inched around me and faced Arrow. "Don't threaten my mate ever again or it'll be the last thing you do."

"Okay, my love, they get the point." I placed my hands on her shoulders and drew her tiny frame against mine.

Saoirse walked in front of Arrow a second before he said anything to Sophia about her threat and took the baby from his arms.

"Here, meet your nephew." Saoirse thrust the baby into Sophia's arms before she objected.

One second the room was hostile with tension, the next Sophia gazed into the baby's tiny face, and she cooed to him in a soothing sound almost resembling her purr. My heart warmed with a babe in her arms and want coursed through my veins to put a baby in her womb.

She bounced the baby as he gurgled back at her as though talking to her in his own language. Sophia giggled. I'd never heard her giggle before, so I cocked an eyebrow in surprise. The baby giggled too as Sophia cooed back.

"He wants to meet his uncle." She handed me the baby.

I held him awkwardly. How did a little being like him hold so much Fae power in his body? The power hummed inside him like a beacon to my power. As a male Fae royal, he possessed the same powers as me.

The baby gargled at me.

Sophia laughed and cupped the back of his head.

"He wants you to hold him closer." She urged my arms to my body bringing the baby to my chest.

"You can understand him?" Saoirse asked, stepping beside us.

"No." She smiled. "His gurgles are incoherent, but his voice is strong in his mind and fully developed waiting for his body to catch up."

"Wait," Arrow said, slipping an arm around Saoirse's waist. "You can hear his thoughts?"

"Jaguar shifters are telepathic," I said as I bounced the baby who fidgeted his arms and legs. "But I only thought your telepathy worked with other jaguars?"

"Yes, jaguars, our mates, and shifter young. Their minds broadcast loud and clear when you can hear thoughts."

"He wants his uncle Sledge now. He says you're holding him wrong."

Sledge stood and walked over to us.

"Come here, little buddy. They don't know what you like do they?" Sledge said as he placed the baby high on his shoulder and bounced him.

The baby gurgled.

"What did he say?" Saoirse asked.

"He's happy now and wants a nap."

Sledge bounced the baby to sleep on his shoulder.

"Amazing," Saoirse said, taking her child and placing him in a cradle nearby. "A mother sure could use you around to help."

"I can't stay." Sophia peered at me with distress in her green eyes.

"Aye, I'll have to return her to the Amazon soon. Her people need her."

"You have people?" Sledge asked, reclaiming his seat next to Briana.

"I have a colony of jaguar shifters I oversee."

Sledge and Arrow exchanged a glance.

"It's more than that, my love. She's their queen."

Briana and Saoirse gasped.

"Are wolf shifters telepathic too?" I asked.

"No, but they can detect lies," Saoirse said.

"Interesting." I rubbed my jaw. "So, you comprehended Sophia was lying when she said she oversaw her colony?"

"Yeah," Sledge said. "It was almost the truth but there was a ring of a lie in there."

"I'll have to remember you can sense lies," Sophia said.

"Don't worry, I still forget." Saoirse laughed. "Come sit down and tell me why you're here. Briana said Rian made you spy on me."

Sophia glared at me.

I brushed a soothing hand down her hair. "Sophia offered to patrol the area sometimes since she was aware of how worried I was about you being here alone."

"I'm not alone. I have Arrow. And Sledge, and the entire wolf pack. Briana comes by too."

"Still, you're separated from your family and other Fae. As your eldest brother, I worry." I drew Sophia closer to my side and inched us onto the sofa at the opposite end of the furniture to the others. "We both do."

Sophia cleared her throat. "I need to head back soon."

"Aye." I agreed. "I'll get to the point. Magic protects the location you gave birth. Do you know who created the barrier?"

Fae were experts at magical barriers, but other supernatural creatures used them too. We all used them as protection. Barriers were near impossible to breach and as such only those with immense powers could build them. Whoever built the one around the waterfall must be powerful and someone with that much power was a being I needed to talk to because if they could secure a waterfall, would they be able to secure our spring?

"No," Sledge said. "It's always been that way, the same with the town."

"Before your time then. I'd like to visit the area."

"Go right ahead." Sledge waved his hand at the door. "Sophia should know the way."

Briana nudged Sledge with her elbow. "We'll all go. It's important. I can sense it."

"Okay, okay." Sledge stood and held his hand out to Briana.

She took his hand like the princess she was in her floaty green dress and rose to her feet. Arrow scooped the sleeping baby up and placed him in a harness on his back with only a small murmur of protest from him. I rose at the same time as Sophia. She slipped her hand into mine and let me lead her out of the door. A swift breeze had picked up in our short time inside the cabin. Leaves blew across the dirt and gathered around the wheels of the trucks.

"Shit," Sledge said. "We may need to be on standby."

"Yeah," Arrow agreed.

"Standby for what?" I asked.

"A wildfire," Arrow said. "We're firefighters."

"Don't concern yourself with fire. If one starts, I'll put it out."

"Rian, no." Saoirse grabbed my other hand. "Father was so upset with me when I stopped a wildfire with my powers and found me mated to a wolf shifter that he imprisoned me."

"Father did what?" I ground my teeth. Surely, I'd heard wrong. He'd put his daughter in the dungeon?

Saoirse glanced away. "It... he was upset."

"'Tis no excuse, Saoirse."

"Besides." She grinned. "I bested him with our water swords afterward."

"You bested Father in a sword fight?"

She nodded.

"The surprises keep coming in this realm." I chuckled.

Our group walked through the forest, our footsteps falling into a natural rhythm as the slight track led us deeper into the dense eucalyptus trees and wattle bushes with tiny yellow flowers. After a while, Arrow led us to a circle of trees. A small gap in the base of the thick green bushes was the only entrance. Arrow ducked through the gap. Saoirse followed, as did Sledge and Briana.

"Only one way to see what's inside." Sophia followed them.

I scanned the forest around us searching for a danger that wasn't there. If the three predators who were in our group didn't sense any threat, then why did I? Nothing moved or claimed my attention. If someone or something was out there, they'd hidden well. I crouched and shimmied through the gap since my powers wouldn't part the foliage.

As I stood on the other side of the barrier a streaming waterfall fell over a rockface into a glistening pool below. No sound had alerted me to the presence of the waterfall on the other side of the trees but now it cascaded with a tempo that filled the air with the noise. What a powerful barrier there must be around this water. *Why?*

Saoirse held her arms out. "Isn't the waterfall beautiful?"

"Aye," I agreed. The sparkling blue water falling over the ledge of rocks into the pool underneath was charming. Almost how I remembered our Spring of Life flowing with force and power. This place possessed a tiny portion of those. Waving my hand, I called a droplet of water to my fingertip and placed it in my mouth. I'd expected more from the water. A power like our spring but alas, this water was lacking.

"It's not the source of our spring," Saoirse said. "I would have sensed that, but I am drawn to this place."

"You love water, Saoirse. You honed your power over water, of course, you're drawn here."

"I sense something here too," Briana said. "And I perfected my power over plants."

I turned to my mate. "What do you sense?"

CHAPTER FIVE
SOPHIA

IT DIDN'T SURPRISE ME Rian asked for my opinion. He always did. No matter how separate we were in location, our mate bond always connected us. I wanted to speak into his mind, but four sets of eyes stared at me awaiting my answer.

I padded to the boundary of the pool and squatted, sending my extra sensitive senses of vibrations out. Nothing bounced back to me. This place was strange in the way someone had used magic to seclude the area. I stripped my clothes, needing my jaguar form to delve deeper into whatever was hidden here. Rian's sisters didn't bat an eyelash at my nakedness, but the wolf shifters wisely glanced away. Shifter rules were the same no matter which species we shifted into that staring was not allowed in our naked forms and we were to be respected even when naked.

Fur and claws burst from my body in a blinding flash of ebony power. I stood on my paws, letting the vibrations from the water hitting the pool soak into me. My whiskers twitched as the droplets misted the air. I padded around the edge of the pool and closer to the waterfall, drawn by the surge of water. My tail swished as the vibrations grew stronger. I jumped into the water and swam toward the pounding spray. Ducking underneath the deluge, I clambered onto the rock ledge behind the falling water. Through the muted spray I found the others where I'd left them. Rian would let me investigate by myself. He understood I worked better alone when as a jaguar.

I focused on the wall. The gushing water had worn away the smooth rocks over years. Each second I was here, my senses flared even though my gaze found nothing. I padded along the ledge, back and forth. My whiskers twitched with each step as did my tail. *What was here? And where?* I shifted shape and ran my hands along the wall searching for an anomaly that shouldn't be there, but I found nothing. Tipping my head back, I gazed up, taking in the fall's height. The sun glinted through the water sending rainbows across the rock face, but then a red flare sparkled.

"There."

"What's there, my love?"

"I don't know yet. Give me a few minutes to climb the rock face."

"Do you need assistance from my powers?"

I considered saying no and climbing the wall with my claws, but the smooth surface wouldn't give me much purchase. Plus, I wanted my mate by my side.

"Yes."

Rian appeared by my side, my clothes in his arms. I dressed in the damp material and pointed up.

"Watch. There's a red flare now and then."

Rian followed my instructions and peered up. We watched and waited while the rainbows danced for us. The colors were exquisite. No wonder his sister loved this place. Even with no Fae power over water, I found the place extraordinary.

"I saw nothing," Rian said. "I can't make out what it is up there from down here though."

"Me either. So up I go."

He brandished his hands and two thick vines slithered down the rock face, landing at our feet.

"Up we go."

"Your family won't follow us?"

"No, they wouldn't risk leaving Saoirse and the baby."

I placed a quick kiss on his lips and hauled myself up the vine, grateful his powers were so astounding he called plants to his aid whenever he needed.

"I would have floated us up on air." He grunted as he climbed beside me. "But I figured you'd prefer to climb."

"Too right." I grinned. "As much as I love your powers, we don't know what we'll find."

"Mate, you wound me by insinuating my powers won't handle whatever is in the rocks."

I stopped myself from rolling my eyes. I never intentionally insulted his powers, but it was funny when I did so on accident.

Hand over hand I pulled myself up while using my legs in a monkey grip to climb the vine. Now and then, the red glinted as though drawing us to it. A beacon to something big. When we reached the place where the red blinked, we stopped. There was nothing on the wall. No red marks or gemstones to say this was the place. It made little sense. I peered up again. The red glinted higher.

"How is that possible?" I asked. "It shouldn't have moved."

"No."

We exchanged a concerned glance but then nodded in agreement we should continue.

"Your family is probably worried," I said.

"They needn't be." Rian's muscles bulged as he hauled his body up the rock face.

"Stop!" I yelled as his hand almost touched the bright red flare against the rockface.

The spot glowed so brightly just above our heads, the red was almost blinding.

"What do you sense?" he asked. "I see nothing."

My skin twitched. I hovered a hand over the shining light.

"It's cold, but I sense nothing bad coming from it."

"I trust your senses."

I shoved my hand into the light before I rethought my action. My hand felt like it was freezing to the point it'd snap off. I almost cried out, but my fingertips touched a lever. Grasping the handle, I pulled. To my right where Rian hung, the walls creaked and groaned as a circular rock rolled to the side revealing a tunnel into pitch-black darkness. The red light stopped glowing, and warmth returned to my hand. I swung into the entrance of the tunnel and landed in a crouch. No booby traps exploded from the walls, but I stayed low.

"Are you coming?" I called, shimmying along the ground, getting a sense of the tunnel.

"You and your love of caves." Rian huffed.

A second later, he landed beside me. He shot me a grin then used his power to make bright orange flames flicker over his hand.

"You're handy to have around." I scooted closer to him as he waved his hand up and down the tunnel walls.

"You're so funny." He lifted his other hand. "This hand isn't busy right now. I could always pinch your bottom."

"Hey." I rolled over on the ground to the other side of the tunnel.

Rian laughed and followed me. Pinning me to the tunnel floor with his body, he grinned down at me. His fire hand was next to my head, but I didn't fear that he'd singe my hair. No, he was always in control.

"Where do you think the tunnel leads?" I asked before I let my desire for my mate take hold with his body stretched over mine.

"I guess we'll find out." He rolled off me and stood.

I sprang to my feet. "Step slowly and carefully. There might be traps."

"I'll lead since I have the light."

"Your highhandedness comes through sometimes."

"Wait until you meet my father."

"I'm not sure I want to." A shudder ran down my back thinking about what Saoirse said. I'd witnessed Rian's memories, so I'd seen the Fae King wasn't an evil person, but he'd done some questionable things. That was for sure.

"My love." Rian sighed.

"Sorry, I didn't mean that. You know I hope we'll be together properly one day."

"As do I."

"Let's leave this discussion at that for now and concentrate on this tunnel."

"You're right." His lips thinned. "Stay close."

He placed one foot in front of the other, pausing after each step to sweep the floor, walls, and ceiling of the tunnel with his glowing fire hand. Nothing appeared out of the ordinary, so we moved forward. The process was slow, and time trickled away like the grains of sand in an hourglass. Pace by pace, the tunnel veered uphill until the muscles in my legs were aching with the incline. Rian extinguished his flames.

Up ahead, a glow of golden light shone.

"Daylight or something else?" he whispered.

Once again, I sent my senses out letting the jaguar part of me experience the currents in the air.

"Daylight," I said when I was certain there was nothing magical up ahead.

He brought the flames back to his hand. The flare of his power sent my body tingling. He pinched my bottom as he'd threatened to do earlier. I jumped forward and swatted his hand.

"Keep your hands to yourself, mate. Until later, that is." I winked.

He laughed and stepped in front of me once again. Each step closer to the golden glow revealed the tunnel led outside. Into what, we weren't sure. Soon we'd find out though. Maybe we'd even discover who put the barrier around the waterfall up here. We paused at the edge of the tunnel and peered outside. A forest of vibrant green, moss-covered Redwood trees greeted us. Birds chirped on their branches. The sun glowed through the canopy. The leaves rustled in the breeze.

"I sense nothing," I said before Rian asked.

"Out we go then."

We walked out of the long tunnel into the daylight. To the left was a dirt path leading through the forest.

"Keep going or go back and tell the others?"

"Keep going. If the wolves had found this, they would have told us. We can't stay here too long, and I want to see where this leads before we leave."

"Right." I stepped forward.

He snagged my hand in his.

"You don't need to lead out here, Mr. Fire Hand."

He extinguished his flames and caught my waist with his palm and drew me toward him. His mouth descended on mine, and he kissed me as though I was the very air he needed to survive.

"What was that for?" I asked.

"Because you may not need me, but you want me, and I was reminding you."

I cupped his jaw. "I need you."

"You don't act as though you do."

"If I don't act it, it's because—shit—what was that?"

A loud gong reverberated through the forest. I clutched Rian's shirt in my hands and hung onto the fabric.

"I'm assuming someone knows we're here." His lips pursed.

The chime rang for so long, I didn't think the noise would end, but the sound petered out to silence, and the forest resumed its noises once again.

"I think we should go back." I pulled at his shirt.

"Your jaguar didn't like the noise."

"No, the chime made my ears hurt."

"But you sensed no magic."

"No."

"So we proceed."

"Rian, this is ludicrous. We don't know where we are or what we're walking into."

"Mate, I can whisk us away in a heartbeat into the Veil."

I cursed under my breath. "Stubborn male."

He chuckled as we walked down the dirt path into the thickness of the moss-covered Redwood trees to who knows where.

CHAPTER SIX
SOPHIA

"*S*OPH, WHEN ARE YOU *coming home?*" Lazarus, my second cousin, spoke inside my mind.

"*Bit busy right now, Laz,*" I said.

"*You with that absent mate of yours?*"

"I'm right here," Rian said.

"*Shit.*" Lazarus cursed.

I sighed. "*What do you want, Laz?*"

"*We've spotted poachers outside the left quadrant of the north sector.*"

"*Fuck. How many?*"

"*Two.*"

"*If they come in our territory, kill them.*"

"*Will do.*"

"*And, Laz, my relationship is none of your business or anyone else's.*"

"*Sorry, Soph.*"

His voice disappeared from inside my head.

"I don't like him," Rian said.

"He doesn't like you either."

"I'm well aware."

"He and his mother are the last of my family."

"I'm aware of that too."

"But you still don't like him."

"Correct."

"Are you ever going to tell me why?"

"It's a male thing." Rian strode down the path.

I hurried to catch up to him.

"What's that supposed to mean?"

"Don't play dumb when we both know you're not."

"Rian." I huffed. "He's my second cousin."

He shrugged. "You have your senses and I have mine."

"No. I don't believe it."

"Believe what you want. I'm only your mate so what do I know?"

"You're acting jealous for no reason." I tugged on his arm and forced him to stop.

"Am I? Who's the one by your side night and day? Who's the one in your ear day and night? Who's the one saying things about me when I'm not there?"

"He's my general. Of course, he's in communication with me. He handles the patrols of the perimeter and the reports come to me through him." I dug my fingers into his arm. "As for saying things about you, he's only called you my absent mate."

He touched a finger to the side of my head. "Planting seeds of doubt."

"I have no doubts about you." I grabbed his other arm. "You're my fated mate. My everything. I'd never doubt you."

He sighed. "I miss you so much. When I'm not near you, it burns a hole in my chest."

"Rian." I sighed too. "One of us will have to make a choice soon."

"Give me a little more time." He rubbed his forehead.

I drew his hand away and massaged his temples. "All right."

His eyes glittered with the same hope and despair I experienced. I'd give up my home and people for Rian but joining him in the Summer Court would cause him more problems and a greater divide between his family. I didn't want that pain for my mate. My family had a massive rift when my father left my mother for a siren. Sure, he'd claimed to be under the influence of her song, and he'd come crawling back, but the damage had been done and my mother never forgave him. Never let him back into our colony. He'd died a gruesome death at the hands of poachers for his jaguar pelt. Mother blamed herself and while hunting the poachers to exact her revenge she'd ventured into a rogue jaguar's territory. The male jaguar attempted to claim her, but she refused and died while deflecting his advances.

The life of jaguar shifters was often brutal and always bloody.

I realized Rian feared for my life. He'd suppressed the need to voice those concerns to my face, but I caught whispers in his mind when he didn't realize he was speaking to me. If I could assure him I was safe, I would, but no one was safe on Earth. The place was hostile and grew worse each year. I wished I'd lived when the Fae ruled the Earth and we'd all lived in harmony. I held onto the hope Rian would convince his father to let the Fae return. To help us once more.

In silent agreement, we continued along the path. The red trunks of the trees grew taller as though reaching into the sky. White fluffy clouds hung around the green tops of the trees, giving the place an intriguing quality. Bark peeled from the trunks in long strips that flapped in the breeze. My hair whipped around my face, and I gathered the length in a fist and twirled the strands into a knot at the back of my neck. Before us, two great stone pillars of white stone rose on either side of the track appearing out of place at the same time as looking ancient with carved abstract faces in the long columns.

"Where are we?" I scanned to the left and right. I'd never seen columns like these before.

"Earth."

This time I rolled my eyes.

"We didn't pass through a portal to another realm, but I suspect we're in a magic-enhanced dimension."

"Have you seen these before?"

"No." He frowned. "I don't know who made them."

Rian stepped forward toward the giant faces on the columns. Power flared in a rippling curtain of luminous blue between the columns as though an impenetrable gate of magic stood between them. Small dart arrows spurted from the mouth of the statues. I launched myself at Rian placing my body between the danger and him as I tackled him to the ground. At the same time, he used his powers and flung a wall of dirt up from the ground. We lay on the ground in a tangle of limbs, breathing heavily.

"Shit," I said.

"Shite," Rian said at the same time.

We smacked our lips together in a heated kiss.

"I guess there were booby traps in the end," Rian said.

"I like it when I'm right."

We both sat up and dusted the dirt from our clothes. On the ground where the darts had hit were black inky stains. I reached out a hand to touch the closest one.

"Don't do that." Rian snatched my hand back. "We don't know what was in those darts, but it appears to be deadly otherwise the ground wouldn't blacken like that."

"It looks like an oil stain. If they hit us..." I shivered.

"End of the line until we figure out who's protecting what's behind those columns." Rian stood and offered me his hand.

"Let's head back to your family and let them know what we found."

"Which was nothing but more secrets that we don't know if they'll help us."

"It's worth researching though."

"Aye."

We stepped back along the dirt path, being careful where we put each foot and scanning our surroundings to make sure we didn't trigger any other booby traps. I sensed Rian's despair like a black cloud in his head. He'd thought the waterfall was the key to the Spring

Baile even though Saoirse had said it wasn't. I threaded my fingers through his and squeezed. He accepted my offer of comfort like he always did, with the same amount of love in his return caress. We walked inside the tunnel. Rian's power flared and his hand once again became a torch. It always astounded me his flames didn't burn his flesh. His powers captivated me. The tunnel wound down the slope until the rushing of the waterfall echoed into the space. We closed the distance between us and the exit. I was relieved when we reached the ledge behind the waterfall. Rian's vines had disappeared though and the drop to the pool below was too far to jump.

"Okay prince charming, how are we getting down?"

"Who is this prince charming? And where do I find him to challenge him to a duel?"

I laughed. "You're adorable. He's a fairy tale character."

Rian frowned.

"You'd duel with swords for me?" I placed my hands on my hips. "I forget how old you are sometimes."

"This Earth is not like the one I visited in my youth." He wiped a drop of water that landed on my cheek from the spray.

"I remember your memories but it's not the same as living them. I wish I'd known how we all lived together in harmony back then. That I'd lived it myself instead of this unease and division we have now." I clenched my fingers into tight fists. "I'm tired of always fighting and struggling to keep us alive when we should live forever."

He gathered me into his arms. "I'm sorry, my love. My father's choices have affected too many, but he wasn't to know. He was only protecting us."

I nestled my head against his chest and listened to his heart pound with certainty he was right about his father. But while protecting his people he'd destroyed so many other lives. I wasn't sure what I'd say to him when I met him. Perhaps that was another reason Rian prolonged the inevitable of one of us choosing to give up our homes for the other.

A gust of wind lifted my hair that fell out of the knot and circled downward tickling my arms and legs as the air embraced us in a blistery kiss. Our bodies lifted off the ground.

"No, Rian," I gasped as our feet left the ledge.

"It'll be quicker this way."

I buried my face in his chest and squeezed my eyes shut. "I'm a jaguar. I don't fly."

"We're not flying. More like levitating." He chuckled.

"You're lucky I love you."

"I know I am." He kissed the top of my head.

Our feet hit the ground. In reflex, I half-shifted and swiped a claw to scramble back, catching Rian across the face in my haste to lower myself to the ground. My breath came in shallow pants.

"Slower." Rian rubbed my back.

"Why did you hit my brother?" Saoirse squatted in front of me, a blazing blue sword made of water in her hand.

"The jerk made me fly when I hate flying." I sat back on my bottom.

The water sword disappeared from her hand. "Fair enough. Do you want me to hit him too? I haven't enjoyed a good sparring session with him for too long."

I grinned. His sister was just as feisty as me. "Tempting as that is to watch, I don't have the time. Another day?"

"Aye." Saoirse rose and took the restless baby from Arrow. "What were you doing behind the waterfall for so long?"

"Saoirse." Arrow chuckled.

"Oh, no, not that." I blushed.

Rian laughed. I shot him a glare.

"We found a secret tunnel entrance high on the wall," Rian said. "It led us through to another forest. Through the forest was a path. At the end of the path were two great stone columns with faces etched into them. As we got closer, a barrier flared between them, and the faces came alive to shoot darts at us. That was as far as we went."

Briana stepped closer. "Did they hit either of you?"

"No, we're fine," I said. "We agreed we should come back since neither of us wanted to be a pin cushion."

"All this time, that's been up there?" Sledge asked glancing up at the waterfall. "There must be powerful magic to hide all that. Whenever we scout the territory, it's more of the Australian forest up there."

"I've climbed the rockface behind the waterfall and never seen a glowing red light or found a lever," Arrow said.

"It appeared ancient," Rian said. "Whoever is up there doesn't want visitors. The darts stained the ground with blackness."

"But they might know something about our spring," Saoirse said.

"They might." Rian shrugged. "I'll head back home and ask Ciara to research stone columns with faces, darts that stain with blackness, and anyone she thinks might have the power to wield such a place. With any luck, she'll discover something. Maybe even who is up there and how we can let them know we only want to talk and find out if they can help us."

"So much for this place being the key to our spring. I was so certain Saoirse was wrong and the waterfall held our magic," Briana said and let out a long sigh.

"It may well be," Rian said. "We have much to research here and it's the most powerful place we've found surrounding water. This is better than we've found so far."

"You're right. I'd hoped for more right now. I suppose we need patience."

"Aye, we'll find what we're looking for," Rian said. "Are you heading back to the Summer Court soon?"

"In a couple of days." She stepped into the muscular arms of Sledge.

"I'll see you there. I'm leaving now."

"Already." Saoirse pouted. "I miss you all so much."

"We miss you too. Especially Lorcan."

"Tell him to come to visit me then."

"He cannot do so at this time." Rian shifted his feet.

"It was lovely to meet you all," I said, cutting off his sister's interrogation. "But we must go. Poachers are circling my territory and if I don't head back now, then I might lose some jaguars."

"Poachers?" Sledge asked.

"They're just humans trying to make a living the wrong way. We all must make do with what's available to us. Unfortunately, jaguar pelts fetch a lot of money and since they don't know we're shifters, they don't realize who they're killing." I grimaced. "I don't enjoy killing the poachers, but I will."

"What sort of traps do they use?"

"Most use snare traps with nooses made of wire which are very hard to see in the jungle. Others use pit traps with bamboo poles as spikes, but they seldom use them these days. Why do you ask?"

"Someone fatally injured my father by an abrupt fall and a branch almost pierced his heart not too long ago. A crazy wolf shifter female was intent on making me Alpha, so I'd claim her. The whole incident was strange, and we believe she wasn't working alone."

Rian's face hardened. "I thought you were safe here," he hissed.

"I am. Nothing else has happened," Saoirse said.

"I don't like it."

"Neither do I," said Arrow. "But Sledge has locked the town down tight. No one is getting in or out. If someone was helping her, they've either left or they're waiting to free her from the jail cell. We've got wolves watching the place day and night. We'll catch whoever helped her."

"Do regular perimeter checks. Mix up your routine. Set signal trip wires," I said.

"We've done all that," Sledge said. "Plus, we've called in a witch to reinforce our protection barrier spell, but she hasn't come yet. You know how witches are."

"There isn't much else you can do then." I placed a soothing hand on Rian's back. "This is what life is like on Earth now. Your sister has powers. She's surrounded by a wolf shifter pack. She'll manage this world."

Rian's face darkened like storm clouds in the sky. "I dislike it."

He narrowed his eyes at his sisters, then waved his hand and breached the locked Veil with ease. The air shimmered in bronze-gold hues as he took my hand and urged me into the Veil. I caught one last glimpse of his family's faces before the Veil closed on Earth and we stood together in the swirling misty air, the place of magic that separated the two realms and our lives.

CHAPTER SEVEN
RIAN

ANGER AND FRUSTRATION WHIRLED like a thickening storm cloud inside my mind and body. Instead of taking Sophia home as I'd intended, I led us out of the Veil into the Summer Court. The Trembling Giant trees of our forest surrounded us and shielded us from the view of the palace in the distance and even further away from the village. The golden leaves and silvery trunks were a sign we were no longer on Earth and these trees held magic like the rest of the kingdom.

Sophia spun out of my hold. "Where are we?"

"Home," I said, simply. This was the place I called home. The place I wanted her to call home too. And the place she should want to call home.

"Your home? The Summer Court?"

"Aye."

Eyes wide, she stared at the surrounding trees and pursed her lips. She may not be happy about being here, but she appeared intrigued, and I'd take that.

"I've wanted to bring you here for so long."

She lifted her beautiful face from the scenery to stare into my eyes.

"I've longed to walk with you through the forest, around the lake, through the palace, and the rose garden. Most importantly I've wanted to show you our spring and introduce you to my family." I dropped her steadfast gaze.

"Why now?"

I swiped a tongue over my dry lips. The words I was afraid for her safety didn't want to leave my throat. I was a powerful Fae prince with phenomenal powers, but I was worried about my mate being on Earth by herself without me. Even more so after what the others said today.

"After all these years, why now? Was it what happened today?"

I shrugged and let my power coat my hands trying to decide what to do with them. Draw a bouquet from the soil or a swarm of butterflies. Coax a flame into a small firepit so I'd draw her onto the ground and wrap her in my arms. Or make rain fall so I'd create a shelter from giant leaves we'd huddle under and pretend the rest of the two worlds didn't exist. That they were no longer out of harmony and at risk of perishing.

Our problems were bigger than I'd first thought. So narrow-minded of me to think of only the Fae and how we were suffering when the other supernatural creatures on Earth were perishing alongside the humans. This had to stop.

"Aye," I said because even though I thought all those things, I couldn't say them to her.

"I can't be here right now, Rian. You know that." She crossed her arms over her chest.

"I want you here. With me."

"Don't go all caveman idiot on me." Her fingers tapped on the soft skin of her arm.

I cocked an eyebrow.

"You can't throw me over your shoulder, hide me in a cave and call me yours forever."

A smirk stretched my lips. "Now that you mention it, a cave sounds like a wonderful idea."

She shook her head. "Men are boneheads."

"Men plural or just me?"

She laughed. My mate never stayed mad at me. It was one of the many things I loved about her. From her expressive green eyes to her kissable lips, to the scent that was all hers when I'd aroused her. Then there were the curves of her body, the softness of her skin, and the silkiness of her hair. The soft moans and purrs she made when I pleasured her. My cock hardened in an instant.

"Stop right there." She held up her hand. "You can forget those thoughts you're having and take me home to Earth."

"What thoughts would those be, my mate?" I inched closer toward her.

Her eyelids dropped, and she narrowed her eyes to slits. "You know what I'm talking about."

"I dare say I do, but please enlighten me."

"Sexy thoughts." She huffed.

"Hmm, you can do better. Dia, I can do better." I stepped closer until my breath gusted over her hair, but I didn't touch her. She loved the anticipation. The build-up to her release. "Thoughts of laying you out spread-legged so I can bury my face in your sweet arousal."

Her breath hitched and goosebumps pebbled over her skin.

"How I'd lick your little clit until it was hard and engorged."

She blew out a long breath gusting the warmth of her exhale over my chest making me ache to have her touch me. Perhaps I liked the anticipation too.

"Then I'd bury my tongue inside, swirl it in all the wetness you'd created just for me, your mate." I brushed a fingertip down the side of her face.

She shivered. Her green eyes grew luminous, and her scent flourished with arousal.

"When you cover my face with your lusty arousal, I'd stop."

"Stop?" She blurted out so lost in the scene I'd created she'd forgotten we were in the Summer Court.

"You want to go to Earth, remember? To the place that tries to kill you." I gathered her hand in mine and waved the Veil open with my other hand. "Instead of staying here with your mate and being pleasured for eternity."

The Veil parted, and I drew her inside the swirling mist, my anger growing with every second we were on our way back to Earth. To the place I was beginning to understand why we'd left. She squirmed in my hold, but if I let go, she wouldn't make it out, she'd be stuck in this in-between part of our worlds. My hand tightened around hers to the point she stopped moving. I walked us out of the Veil into the thick jungle of her home in the Amazon.

Up above us sat the colony's tree houses. So high they were supposed to be safe from predators. But from what I'd learned today, I doubted their height would stop a human from hurting them if that was what they desired.

Movement stirred as her crew spotted our presence.

"Soph." Laz waved from the balcony of a treehouse and scrambled to the rope ladder.

"You're such an ass," she said into my mind.

"What did I do?" I asked innocently.

"You know what you did. You showed me the beauty of the Summer Court. Turned me on. Then brought me back here where I'll be off killing humans instead of having you between my legs relieving this ache."

I chuckled.

Laz scooted to a stop in front of us. The adoration for his second cousin always made me grind my teeth. Today was no exception as he gazed at Sophia with obvious devotion. With my anger and frustration still raging through me, I could call a fire sword to my hand and cleave his head off in one swipe. Tempting. But Sophia wouldn't understand. I barely understood the need to end his life. He'd done nothing wrong and yet he set my powers tingling through my body.

"About time you got home," Laz said. "We're heading out now to deal with the poachers."

"Good timing," Sophia said, looking anything but pleased about the timing.

"Well, I'll leave you to your—" I waved my hand to encompass the entire jungle.

"Rian." She grabbed my shirt in two fists and pulled me toward her face.

My mate kissed me with a desperation I experienced. The lustful longing of wanting to do what I said. The urge to keep her safe but realized I couldn't, not when she wasn't by my side. Two halves trying to be whole but failing all the time.

Laz grumbled under his breath.

I opened my eyes to stare at him while still kissing Sophia. I claimed her with my mating mark, but every time I was around him, I experienced the desire to mark my claim in any way. Ridiculous since Laz and Sophia were related. Immature too. But instinctual. I'd run with those instincts.

Laz met my stare and flicked back his thick black hair. Every jaguar shifter in Sophia's colony was black. Not one jaguar exhibited tan-colored fur with dark rosettes, they all boasted a melanistic black coat. I saw the same ebony color in their hair. Even my blinding silver blonde hair grated on my nerves that I wouldn't be able to hide in the shadows with Sophia in the way her second cousin could.

I broke the kiss before I turned into a feral animal and claimed Sophia's willing body on the ground in front of Laz and no doubt the rest of the colony. What we had was more precious than a display of dominance, but Laz's jaguar was close to the surface and my powers were going wild.

Sophia cupped both cheeks with her hands and pecked my lips. "Hurry back this time."

"I will." I swiped a thumb over her kiss-ravaged lips. "Stay safe."

I let my raging powers unlock the Veil. At least this way they had an outlet for the emotions storming their way through my body. I stepped into the bronze-gold mist and whispered into her mind, *"You and I have unfinished business."*

"Yes, you with your face between my legs."

She blew me a kiss. I could no longer see the beauty of my mate after the Veil closed, or the cheeky smile on her face and the flush of arousal on her cheeks. I longed to see her every day of my life.

I'd had enough of putting everyone else's needs before mine. *When would I ever be able to have a life of my own?*

CHAPTER EIGHT
RIAN

I REAPPEARED IN THE forest whence we left. The place
was empty without my mate by my side. Perhaps that
was me. My chest ached like half my heart was missing.
I walked through the forest startling a snoozing unicorn
in a thick clump of undergrowth into flight through the
forest. The creature's hooves flew across the ground
sending up sparks of glittering gold in its wake. Humans
believed them to be mythical creatures now, as they did
us. They had lost so much on Earth since we left.

The unicorn's white tail fluttered like a trail I should
follow. I cocked my head to the side and stepped in the
hoofprints. It littered each half-moon imprint in the soil
with gold dust. Such special creatures would be worth a
fortune to humans these days with the amount of gold
they left in their wake. It was in their best interest they no
longer lived on Earth. So many mixed emotions churned
inside my stomach. We were safe here but... we weren't
free or perhaps I should say free to live how we wanted.

After hearing what I did today, I empathized with Father. Understood him more than I ever had. Our fated mates meant everything to us and the driving urge to keep them safe was hard to live with when you possessed so much power inside you. I flung a surge of power at a flock of birds. They burst into flight in the sky, ducking and weaving through the fluffy white clouds in a dazzling dance. I added a rainbow to the sky. With a surge of power, I sent a tree to grow another six feet into the sky. Then I added a wind to sing a song through the leaves. Together the elements made a spectacular display. One I'd wanted to show my mate. Yet, she left. Had wanted to leave.

She tore at my heart every time we parted. Ripped the organ to shreds and left it a bleeding mess inside my chest. *Why wouldn't she pick my world to live in?*

I called my power back, settling everything to the way it was. The release of energy helped to relieve the tension in my powers and body, but my churning emotions still didn't dissipate. I gave up following the unicorn, for he'd only lead me around the Summer Court on a wild chase. They were elusive creatures. My youngest sister, Roisin, boasted a way with them as had Briana's daughter before the Trappers had murdered her. Such a sad time those first years after the Trapper burnings. Each year the sadness eased, but the emotion would never leave us. The pain was a part of all of us now. A pain we needed to learn from and not hide from.

In the distance, the impressive library rose through the scenery. The building was almost a palace itself, with a spire for the entrance and a wing to either side. In the left wing, there were ancient scrolls and text of the Fae. In the right wing were the books of the humans that magically appeared. I made my way up to the teal green entrance door. Was there a similar library on Earth? Somewhere with a wing of books about the Fae?

The door swung open with ease as though it expected my entrance. I walked inside the spire. Sunlight streamed through the many windows and glinted off the gold-foiled-covered books. This was the display section, and the librarian let no one touch these tomes unless under direct supervision. Ciara had searched every one of these books in here first before progressing onto the left wing.

I swung left and ventured into the Fae library. Rows upon rows of books stretched from the floor to the ceiling. Carved wooden shelves held the display like a lover's embrace. Flowering pink blossom trees adorned the place. Even nature needed to thrive inside here. I almost tiptoed down the long corridor where I spotted Ciara hunched over a desk. Beside her sat Malachi, her best friend, and the man I suspected who loved my sister but was too scared to tell her.

Each quiet step brought me closer. Malachi lifted his head having picked up on my presence. He inched away from Ciara on the long wooden log bench seat they sat on. On the table laid multiple books across the smooth polished wood all were open to various pages. Ciara wrote on a parchment beside her.

"Good afternoon," I said, sliding onto the seat opposite them.

Ciara jerked her head up. "Rian." She dropped the feathered quill on the parchment leaving a splatter of ink over her writing. "Fiddlesticks." She scooped up the quill and returned it to the pot. Then she wiped the parchment and smeared the ink. She cursed in a more colorful word that my mother would not approve of.

I chuckled.

She grinned and wiped her face smearing the ink over her cheek.

"Oh, Ciara," Malachi said, extracting a handkerchief from his shirt pocket and tilting her chin to the side so he could wipe the ink away. "What am I going to do with you?"

Ciara smiled and batted her eyelashes.

Did I just witness my sister flirting with her friend?

Dia, help me.

I cleared my throat. "I've returned from Earth, and I met with Saoirse and her child."

"You did." Ciara jumped out of her chair. "I'm so jealous. Is he cute? Of course, he is. Does he look like us or like a wolf?"

I laughed, as did Malachi.

"Wolf shifters look human unless they shift into wolves," I said. "He has our coloring. Pale blonde hair. Blue eyes with an indigo rim. He's a little Fae royal."

"Oh." She sat back on the bench and placed her chin in her hands. "I want to meet him."

"Soon." I nodded. Ciara had never been to Earth. She was itching to go to experience everything she'd read about in books. "First, I need you to research something for me."

She sighed. "What is it this time? I can't find any reference to the origins of our Spring Baile here."

"There's a place on Earth near where Saoirse lives. A waterfall surrounded by a magical force field. It might be a protection spell by a witch or more. Inside there's a hidden tunnel that's an entrance to a place with statue pillars that shoot darts."

Malachi's back straightened as he sat up on the bench.

"Do you know something?"

"There was a book Ciara was reading. Where was it?" He spun on the seat and gazed at all the bookshelves. "Shite, I don't remember which section the book was in, but it mentioned stone pillars with faces shooting darts."

"I didn't say they had faces."

"No, you didn't." Ciara jumped off the seat. "We'll find the book."

"I'd appreciate that." I stood too. "Let me know as soon as you find it."

"Rian? What do you think it means?"

"Apart from someone wanting to hide?" I shrugged. "It could mean anything."

"But if this spot drew Saoirse, then it has something to do with her power over water?"

"Don't get your hopes up."

Ciara's face went from smiling to sad. Her eyes took on a sheen that wasn't from the sunlight coming in through the windows.

"At least until we know more."

I gave her a crumb. Something to hold on to. Malachi whispered in her ear, and they strode over to a section of shelving. Sensing I'd lost them to their research, I left the library. The afternoon sun was lowering in the sky almost to the point a glorious sunset would paint the horizon. I turned my back on it. Nothing was beautiful without my mate. Darkness was my constant companion without Sophia near.

The walk to the palace was quiet. A few Fae stopped picking berries in the berry fields to wave at me. I nodded my head in their direction but kept walking as I was in no mood for idle chit-chat. As though sensing my mood even from a distance, they put their heads back down to work. Up ahead, the palace rose like a welcoming beacon.

As a Fae royal, they tasked us with protecting the Spring Baile in the heart of the palace. Something I'd never considered going against. The honor I upheld even though we weren't protecting the spring from whatever was ailing it right now. We were failures and failing more each day. Father must see we needed to change. Otherwise, we'd be stuck in an oasis but would die of mortality once the spring stopped in its entirety.

No Fae wanted that.

The double doors opened at my approach. Grier, Father's oldest aide gave me a stern nod. I tipped my head in greeting and continued my way deeper into the palace. To the one place where this all mattered.

To the spring.

CHAPTER NINE

SOPHIA

RIAN WAS ANGRY. So was I. He'd taken me to the Summer Court without my permission. He'd turned me on, then left me wet and aching. I might kick his shin when he returned before I pulled him in for a hungry kiss. Whenever that would be.

I could reach for his mind. Talk to him that way and I wanted to, but I needed to concentrate on the here and now. On the poachers threatening what we had left of my jaguar colony. After a debriefing with Laz and another six jaguars, Ana, Camila, Miguel, Jose, Samuel, and Cornelius, my most lethal and trusted soldiers, going on the poacher hunting mission, we shed our clothes and shifted.

It was against most wishes of my people that I went on these hunts. They considered me the embodiment of the jaguar shifter species. Our colony only saw me this way. The rest of the solitary jaguar shifters couldn't give a damn I was the queen. They considered themselves a law of their own. Most were bachelor males too wild in their jaguar half to submit to a female. The males were stronger than me physically, but strength wasn't what made me queen. The desire to look after our people put me in this place. A desire passed down through generations to my line of mothers to daughters. When I gave birth to a daughter, she too would be a queen one day. Even though jaguar shifters stopped aging at twenty-five years old, didn't succumb to illness, boasted phenomenal healing rates, and healed cuts, broken bones, and other injuries. We couldn't heal ourselves from a fatal wound to the head or heart.

Some supernatural creatures survived even those but not us. It was why I came on these missions. Over the years, the poachers progressed from drop traps, to snare traps, and some even used high-powered rifles. Those were few since they cost a lot of money, but we could never be too careful.

We spanned out and slinked through the jungle. Fronds of the ferns tickled my sides. Leaves flicked droplets of water onto my head from up above as the last shower of rain left a reminder we were in the humid jungle. This place was so different from the forest in Australia. The forest there almost seemed dry in comparison. Up ahead the scent of the poachers drifted on the wind.

I curled my lip, pausing my steps, getting a taste and sense of the men waiting to capture and kill us.

"Three men," Las said through our mind link.

"I can scent two."

He stepped out of the thick undergrowth in his massive jaguar form. Paws digging into the damp soil, he paused beside me and curled his lip.

"Two up ahead. Where's the third?"

He sent the message out to the rest of our party. Everyone paused, searching for the other man with their noses and eyes, but not one of us sighted him.

"I say we pull back until they're all together," I said.

"But we have two right there," Laz said. He sniffed the air. *"They're cooking dinner, so they're preoccupied and won't sense us coming."*

"True."

"Come on, Soph, it's not like you to hesitate."

Had I let Rian's worry seep into my subconscious? I wouldn't normally call for a pull back when everything was in our favor. The men weren't expecting an assault from multiple jaguars.

"Why isn't the other man with them?"

"He's probably checking the traps or setting more. They know we like to hunt at night."

"They do." I growled softly. These men were a plague on our species. One that needed to be wiped out before they eliminated us. *"Head in slowly. Quietly. I want eyes and ears on everyone at all times. Four in. Four as lookouts. You know the drill."*

"Let's go," Laz rumbled.

Laz, Cornelius, Samuel, and I inched forward. Freeze framing in the way cats do when stalking prey. Not a hair or whisker twitched on us as each small, padded step closer to the camp brought us within striking range.

One man bent over the fire, stirring the food in the pot. The other man sat on the ground, drinking from a canteen, and glancing nervously over his shoulders into the dark forest. He wouldn't spot us. We were too well camouflaged in this twilight. The growing shadows of the night would envelope us and claim us as theirs. Creatures of the night. Hunters on the prowl.

His buddy spoke and handed him a bowl of food. We pounced, startling the men into yelling, and throwing the bowls. The man on the log toppled backward in his fear. Laz latched onto his throat before a garbled scream could rent the air. The other man reached for a gun a second before Samuel clamped on his arm. He jerked him back but not before he fired a shot. The bullet struck the solid trunk of a Mahogany tree. Cornelius lunged at the man and ended his life with a rake of his claws down his chest and abdomen. My tail swished as I surveyed the scene. Not one man let me in on the action.

My annoyance must have flickered through my mind because Laz dropped the man and kicked dirt and leaves over his body while curling his lip at me.

"We should hide before the other poacher returns. He's bound to have heard the shot," I said.

"Or we wait right here and swarm him," Laz said.

"Stop being a fool," I hissed.

He puffed up his chest and flicked his tail.

I lifted my chin in the air and glowered.

Cornelius and Samuel slinked into the bush.

"You're no fun anymore, Soph, not since you mated with the Fae."

"What's he got to do with this?"

"You used to be bold and willing to take on the world, but now you want us to cower."

"There's nothing wrong with using our skills to defeat our opponents."

"We're the superior species over humans. I'm tired of living like we're not."

"We're all tired of living like this."

I lowered my chin. I understood his frustration.

The click of the gun's trigger registered in my ears a moment before the gunpowder scent exploded in the air along with the bullet. I staggered into Laz. A bullet hit me in the side. My legs went weak as though they no longer possessed any feeling. I fell to the ground, knocking the breath out of my lungs.

A jaguar's roar exploded in the air. Then another and another. Soon the screams of the man dying rippled through the thick air, but his death didn't stop the pain in my side or the sticky wetness of my blood seeping through my fur and pooling beneath my body.

"Fuck, Soph, don't shift," Laz said. "I'll carry you back to our priestess. She'll get the bullet out, then you can heal."

Laz scooped me up into his arms. I didn't have the strength to even whisper in his mind I doubted I'd heal from this wound.

Each step through the jungle jostled my body in Laz's arms. The pain flared like a red-hot poker in my side, making my breathing labored. The air seemed like it lacked oxygen as I struggled to maintain my breathing.

Every inhale seared my flesh. Every exhale felt like my last. On and on the pain roared through my body. Laz mumbled the entire time. His words were incoherent through the rushing noise in my ears.

Darkness descended. The shadows wanted to claim me forever. I struggled to keep my eyes open because if I gave into the heavy pull of my eyelids, then that would be the end. My life would cease and with it The Queen of the Jungle would be no more. What would happen to my people? I couldn't leave them.

And my mate.

Rian.

I clung to the image of him in my mind. His silvery blond hair, his intense blue eyes, and the eerie yet beautiful indigo rim around them entranced me forever. The way he loved me for my feistiness. Accepted me as a queen. A mate he'd endure the absence of, doing the right thing for both of us. For our people.

What would happen to him if I died?

"We're going up the ladder now, Soph," Laz said, as he jostled me onto his shoulder.

I cried out in agony, almost passing out. Almost shifting into a woman in his arms. I maintained my jaguar shape only through sheer grit and determination I'd live to see Rian again. To tell him I loved him. To give him...

"Bring her to me," Saltine, our priestess, said.

"Get the bullet out," Laz said, his voice a deep growl as he lowered me to the floor.

"Hold her down. This is going to hurt," Saltine said.

Laz pinned my head to the wooden floor. Others pinned my legs, but my vision was too hazy for me to make out who was holding me down.

Saltine's face peered into my eyes. "Some things need to happen."

If I was in human form, I'd ask her what she meant, but since I wasn't, all I did was blink. She moved to my side and poured a liquid over my coat that burned like she was stripping fur and skin from my body. I squirmed but all the hands and arms, even body weight held me down.

A sharp pain gouged into my side. I howled as Saltine dug deep into my flesh.

With a triumphant smile, she sat back, her hand coated in blood, my blood, to show me the small bullet. She placed her other hand on my head.

"I'll give you an elixir for the pain. It'll knock you out so your body can heal. You need to call your mate first."

"Stop wasting time, Saltine, give her the elixir and let her heal," Laz said. "If her damn mate cared, he'd be here with her, not off in Fae land."

I almost shifted to yell at Laz it wasn't Rian's fault he wasn't here, but one tiny movement as I lifted my head almost made me pass out from the pain.

Saltine stood and walked away, her black cloak swirling around her body like a living dark cloud. Moments later, she motioned for Laz to lift my head. She poured the elixir onto my tongue from a tiny glass vial. A warm fuzzy sensation soothed the inside of my mouth and inched its way down my body. Soon there was no pain, and as that registered, my eyes closed as the healing darkness of sleep claimed me.

CHAPTER TEN

RIAN

THE TRICKLE OF THE spring running over the smooth rocks soothed my churning emotions a fraction as I paced in the atrium. My feet padded over the cobblestones with a soft pitter-patter, adding to the cadence of the water. Up above, the fluffy white blooms dangling from the ceiling wafted a sweet scent.

Mother walked into the room. She paused at the doorway, eyeing me with the concerned look only a mother gave her child even if said child was hundreds of years old.

"Between you and your father, you'll wear a groove in the cobblestones."

She continued to a large boulder on the edge of the spring and settled herself as though the hard rock was the most comfortable place to sit.

Patting the skirts of her plum-colored gown she said, "I met your father here."

I paused my pacing and crossed my arms.

"He was so charming, and sweet." She smiled. "Full of confidence too."

"I remember the story of how you met at his two hundredth birthday ball."

"Aye." She dipped her hand into the spring and observed the water stream between her fingers. "His parents wanted him to choose a mate, yet fate sent me his way. I sometimes wonder why, and if he and the Fae would be better off if we'd never met."

"Mother," I scolded. "How could you speak such a thing?"

"'Tis true, is it not?" She lifted her hand and followed the trail of droplets running down her arm. "Your father locked us all in keeping me safe. Mates will do anything for their mate, even to the detriment of others. It's a flaw we all must live with."

I hung my head. I'd done nothing for my mate that would hurt others. If anything, I protected others and hurt my mate. What did that say about me? Am I a terrible mate? Because I was certain Sophia was my fated mate. My powers responded to her mere presence. They'd been eager to mark her as mine. Aye, we were fated.

"You shouldn't blame yourself for your mate's actions," I said. "Father needs to take responsibility. He is the King."

"And you, Rian." She rubbed the spring's water into her hand. "Would you take responsibility for your actions if you were king?"

"Aye, it's the way you raised me."

"Parents can only do so much. Children have a mind of their own. We love and fight for the ones we love. Your father is fighting for me, for all of us. You children have been so hard on him these last few years with the spring's decline affecting our birth rate." She placed her hands in her lap and lifted her gaze to mine. "Don't you believe he's concerned too? That he wants to find a cure?"

I sighed and uncrossed my arms. "Mother, it's not that. We were all shocked he, and you, wanted us to choose mates. Fae all hold fated mates in the highest of regard. We assumed you'd want one for us."

"We want you to be happy. Briana was happy with her chosen mate. Contented until those dreadful Trappers killed him." Her lips formed a tight line as she touched the streak of red hair at the base of her skull. The remnant of how she'd almost died.

I settled on a boulder beside her and patted her hand. "He needs to unlock the Veil. He vanquished the Trappers. Aye, there are other threats on Earth now, but we can defeat those too."

She squeezed my hand. "You've been to Earth?"

I puffed out a breath. "Aye."

"I miss visiting Earth. As lovely as the Summer Court is, Earth was my first home." Her fingers tightened around my hand.

I turned my hand over and squeezed back. The Trappers killed my mother's entire family. She'd loved them as much as I loved my family.

"'Tis different there now."

"In what way?"

"Well, there are many humans and they've built countless houses and buildings out of brick. Tall structures in their cities. Automobiles they drive along paved roads."

She wrinkled her nose. "Sounds dreadful. What of the forests, the beaches, the moors?"

"They're still there, but they've made them smaller. Every time I step onto Earth, I sense the realm struggling and calling to my power to heal it."

"Oh, Rian." She placed her hands over her mouth and stared into my eyes.

"It's not the beautiful place you remember."

She lowered her hands. "I did not know. Why didn't you say anything?"

"You weren't ready to listen, but now Saoirse is living there, you have a reason to want to listen. Besides, we're supposed to be locked in the Summer Court, remember?"

"For good reason too. Humans are despicable."

"Do you want them to suffer for what they did to us?"

"I'm not so cold-hearted toward the humans that I want them to suffer. Not every one of them was intent on trying to take our powers. How could you say such a thing?" She stood and glared down at me. "How could you even think that about me and your father? We may be King and Queen of the Fae and have their best interests at heart, but we've never been about death until we needed to defend ourselves."

"Mother." I stood, palms out pleading with her. "I didn't mean to offend you."

"I've always listened to you when you've spoken to me."

"You have." I sighed. "Perhaps this is my fault too. I should have spoken sooner about the plight of Earth and the supernatural creatures."

"What's wrong with them?" She straightened her shoulders.

"They've been in hiding since we left. The humans feared and despised anyone with supernatural powers after our massacre of the Trappers."

"That's preposterous!"

"Be that as it may, it's true."

"We need to speak to your father. He must have all the information."

"Rian," Sophia whispered.

I tilted my head to the side.

"Yes, my love?"

No answer came back.

"Sophia?"

"Rian, did you listen to me? We need to talk to your father," Mother said.

I held up my finger to my lips.

"What is it?" Mother whispered, glancing around the atrium as though someone was about to jump out at her.

"Sophia, where are you?"

Still, no answer came. The growing unease prickled my skin and sent a flare of power through my limbs. My fingers tingled as I reached for the sealed Veil.

"Rian, where are you going?"

"To Earth, there's something wrong with my mate." I unlocked the Veil and stepped inside the swirling bronze-gold of hues.

"You have a mate!" She screeched. "Wait!"

I didn't wait. There was something wrong with my mate for she always answered me, even in her deepest sleep, she'd whisper huskily into my mind. Soothe me and caress me with her voice. Right now, her voice didn't come. Which meant the worst had happened.

Sophia was dead.

CHAPTER ELEVEN

RIAN

I WALKED OUT OF the Veil into the heart of the Amazon jungle and beneath the tree holding Sophia's abode. Shifters lunged at me in their cat form, snarling and spitting. I dodged their swipes and almost called a sword to my hand, but at the last second, I changed it to a wooden staff.

"Enough," I said, slamming the end of the staff into the ground and making the soil crack.

The palm trees and rubber trees around us vibrated with the force, their lush green leaves rustling as though a gale-force wind blew through them.

The jaguars staggered and shook their heads.

"I'm Sophia's mate. Why are you attacking me? I mean you no harm." My crown of thorns writhed about my head as my power hummed.

Laz landed on his feet before my eyes. I peered up at the long drop from Sophia's tree house to the ground, but what concerned me was the fact he was in her house.

"Where's Sophia?"

"What's it to you?" Laz stalked toward me and shoved me in the chest.

I swung the staff at him on instinct. He lurched out of the way. His dark hair lifted in the breeze as the staff missed his face by millimeters.

"I'm her mate." I twirled the staff in my hand as my jealousy surged to the forefront. "What were you doing in her house?"

"You're no mate," he spat. "Mates stick by their mate's side. If you were any mate, you would have been here when—" he choked on the last word.

"When what?" I shoved the end of the staff at his throat, holding the weapon steady as his Adam's apple bobbed.

"What do you care?" He knocked my staff away.

"No... she's not..."

I couldn't think of the word let alone say it. Every piece of me ached. It hurt in a way I'd never imagined existed. My hands shook as I used my power to disintegrate the staff.

He dropped his chin to his chest and didn't meet my eyes.

Even more dread surged through me. I caught his t-shirt in my fists and lifted him off the ground.

"Tell me."

I almost shook him until his brains rattled inside his head, but smashed brains wouldn't give me the answer I was looking for. It'd be satisfying. Sophia wouldn't like me making her second cousin brain-dead though.

"Laz," I ground out with a long-ingrained patience of a Fae royal. "Where is Sophia?"

"She's up there." He nodded his head at the treehouse. "You're too late."

"No." I dropped him so fast he fell to his knees, his cat reflexes not even having a chance to kick in. "She can't be dead."

Laz snorted. "Jaguar shifters can die, you stupid Fae."

I didn't spare him a second glance as I raced up the rope ladder. Hand over hand, I drew myself up, my feet barely contacting the rungs in my urgency to get to my mate. I launched myself onto the balcony and rushed through the doorway. Sophia lay in the middle of the room in her jaguar form. Around her, a reddish-brown stain surrounded the timber floor.

"Sophia," I gasped, scrambling across the room, and falling to my knees. "No." I touched my fingers to her face. Her fur was soft, but she was cold. Lifeless. I rocked back on my heels. My mate wasn't dead. We hadn't even enjoyed one lifetime together. We'd barely experienced any time together since we met. This was all my fault. I should have been by her side. I should have forsaken my royal duty and my family to be with my mate. *What was the point?* There was none without my mate by my side. Using my power, I called a dagger to my hand, one made like no other. A blade of fire made by Fae power. If I stabbed myself in the heart and left the burning blade buried deep, then I'd succumb to death too, eventually. Fae recovered from wounds but if we burned too long, then we'd die.

I lifted the blade ready to end this misery. One minute without Sophia was one too many.

"I wouldn't do that if I were you," a feminine voice crackled behind me.

A voice I remembered from centuries ago. The voice of our witch seer.

I spun with a start. "Saltine?"

"Yes, boy." Saltine tossed back the hood of her long black cloak.

She hadn't changed one bit.

"Father said you were dead."

"Yes, well, I can't see my fate, so I didn't see the wolf shifter who rescued me coming." She strode closer. "He was a delightful surprise to my life, calling me his mate. He was sweet."

She clamped her hand around mine holding the flaming dagger.

"Let me go." I yanked on my hand, but she sank her nails into my skin, drawing blood under the half-crescent moon shapes.

"Your mate isn't dead. Yet." She flicked her gaze to Sophia. "You have little time to take her to the Summer Court."

"What will that achieve?"

"Boy." She patted my cheek with her other hand. "Your spring has healing properties, does it not?"

"Aye, for the Fae."

"Since you marked her with your mating mark, she's part Fae now too."

"No?"

"Yes."

"But?"

"Do you want to keep up this one-word conversation, or do you want to save your mate?"

My power flared as I called the dagger back. Saltine's hands left my body. I unlocked the Veil in a wild rush, then turned to Sophia and gently scooped her up from the floor. Her head lay limply over my arm. Every muscle in her body seemed nonexistent. She appeared dead, but Saltine said she was alive. I didn't see how when there was no movement from her body. I stepped into the Veil. Her body shifted in my embrace. Fur turned to skin that had lost color to the point she was gray. Her lips were blue. Even the skin surrounding her closed eyes held a blackened hue.

"I gave her a stasis elixir instead of a sleeping one," Saltine called out.

"What does that mean?" I yelled as the Veil closed around us.

But her answer never came, for the lock snapped back in place on Earth and I could only go one way.

To the Summer Court.

CHAPTER TWELVE
RIAN

I BROKE THROUGH THE Veil, stumbling to my knees in my haste to get to the spring. Mother's startled gasp barely registered. I scrambled to my feet, being ever so careful to not drop Sophia. Never in my long life would I'd hurt her, even if I believed Saltine was wrong and my mate was dead. I paused at the edge of the spring, then remember Father soaking Mother in the healing water when the Trappers had almost burned her to death. Without another thought, I strode into the water still dressed and sat. The trickle of the water reached my waist. I touched my lips to Sophia's forehead and lowered her between my legs keeping her head on my lap and letting the water cover her body.

The water turned pink from the dried blood on her body, then the magic of the spring swirled up and over her body, disintegrating the pink into a steaming mist. It floated in the air toward the fluffy white blooms hanging from the atrium ceiling. Every plant cell reached for the mist and drew the water into its stems, leaves, and buds. Sparks of gold rained down from the ceiling, hitting the water and making it clear once more.

"What just happened?" Mother asked, kneeling on a boulder at the edge of the spring.

"I'm not sure." I frowned. "Nothing like this happened when Father soaked you in the Spring."

"Is this your mate?"

"Aye. Sophia. She's a jaguar shifter."

"Oh." Mother rested her head on her hands and peered at my mate closer.

"Are you upset she's not a Fae?" I asked.

"No. That doesn't bother me. You know my family mixed with all sorts. Even humans back before... you know..."

She always struggled to talk about the past.

"Aye." I sighed.

She dipped her hand in the water. "What I meant to say is, you didn't give her a Fae crown when you marked her. Why?"

I ran a damp hand over Sophia's hair. "She's the queen of their people. I didn't want to take that away from her."

"You're giving her a precious gift, Rian, not taking something away from her."

"She might not see it the same way." I cupped the side of her face. She was still pale. Still lifeless. Saltine must have been wrong about our spring.

"What happened to her?"

"I don't even know. I forgot to ask."

Mother chuckled. "The spring will heal her. She's your mate. It'll recognize her."

"Perhaps." I firmed my lips. "Why won't she wake? I need to hear her voice. See her eyes. Have some sign she's not dead."

"She's not dead. Watch. Her chest rises and falls once a minute." She pointed at Sophia.

We sat watching her body in the running water for what seemed like an eternity until I caught the slight rise and fall of her chest.

"There." I sat up straighter.

"Aye." Mother nodded.

Tears threatened the backs of my eyes. I swallowed past the lump in my throat.

I ran my fingers through the strands of her hair as it floated in the water around my legs. My power thrummed to the point I couldn't control it any longer. I dug my fingers into the thick nest of her hair. Swirling bronze-gold colors circled her head as my power flared. I sighed with relief. The release of power had never been so good. So right. On and on my power circled Sophia's head happy to place a royal Fae mark on her crown. Tiny white flowers burst through the black of her hair first. Next came delicate pink blooms. Followed by a soft lavender flower. Tiny light green buds highlighted the blooms. Then an unusual blue flower appeared, larger than the rest and one I'd never seen before.

My mate was gorgeous before but now she was exquisite. A rare beauty of feline suppleness combined with a Fae crown. Why hadn't I bestowed the power upon her head earlier? Because with each passing second her crown sat upon her head the rightness of the moment circled my power, body, and mind.

Mother cleared her throat and stood, her hands dropping on her chest, she sang.

Two hearts,
Weaved as one.
One life,
Combined by two.
Take my hand,
My love.
Take my hand.
Walk with me
On this journey.
Waltz with me
Through the fields.
Take my hand,
My love.
Take my hand.
Breathe for me,
As I breathe for you.
Come to me,
As I am yours.
Take my hand,
My love.
Take my hand.

The unusual Fae power Mother possessed in her voice swirled around us. I sensed the note of healing she'd imbued in the song. The same tone she'd used to help heal us whenever we'd caught the end of a sword in a sparring match. With each note, the color in Sophia's face darkened a fraction. When Mother finished singing, Sophia at least appeared semi-alive instead of dead.

Sophia's dark eyelashes fluttered against her cheeks. "My love?"

Her chest rose higher on a deep inhale.

I held my breath, hoping she'd open her eyes, yet they didn't part.

"Rian." Mother touched my shoulder. "The spring has done all it can. Take her to your room. I'll bring up a dry nightgown for you to change her into."

"She's still not awake."

"Your mate will wake when she's finished healing enough to do so." She squeezed her hand on my shoulder in a comforting touch. "Have faith in your mate. She won't want to leave you."

"I love her so much, Mother, and I never put her first." I hung my head as shame coursed its way through my body.

"Everyone makes mistakes."

The wise words of my mother echoed in my head. I gathered Sophia into my arms and stood. The water sluiced from our bodies as though the spring was calling the precious droplets back. Mother unbuckled her cloak and placed it over my mate's naked body. I strode from the water and headed to my bedchambers through the long marble hallways of the Fae palace. With each step and each breath, I hugged Sophia closer to me. I wouldn't lose her, not when it'd taken so long for me to find her. How I'd gone against my father's wishes that I stay in the Summer Court and broken through the locked Veil. Everything about our meeting should never have happened and yet it did.

Fate brought us together.

Fate would keep us together.

Or I'd follow her wherever she went. She was my heart. My love for all time.

I swung open the thick timber door to my bedchambers and carried Sophia to the bed. Mother knocked on the door and walked inside, placed a nightgown on the bed then left, closing the door behind her. I stripped Sophia out of the damp cloak, letting out a string of curse words when I glimpsed the harsh angry wound on her side. Her skin was pink and puckered. Healed enough to stop bleeding but not so completely healed the scar had disappeared.

On the dark blue bedsheets, she appeared pale again. Not her usual deep coloring. Her chest rose and fell in more regular intervals now but still not in a normal cadence. I eased the white nightgown over her body, almost cracking a smile at seeing her in a Fae gown, albeit a nightgown. The soft fabric covered her naked form in a way that clung to her curves and did nothing to distract from her innate sexiness even though the gown fell around her ankles.

She sure would have something to say about this nightgown when she woke. This time I smiled. Drawing the blanket back, I lifted her into bed, stripped out of my damp clothes and slipped in beside her, and clung to her as though my life depended on it.

It did.

CHAPTER THIRTEEN

SOPHIA

Awareness seeped into my body and mind as the blackness receded. I had been lost in the dark. My body and mind were there in the darkness, but neither moved while I healed. My breathing picked up the pace along with my heartbeat. Tingles started in my fingertips and traveled up my arms, over my shoulders into the base of my skull, sparking my brainwaves back into existence. From there, the sparks flew down my body igniting every cell in my being.

My eyelids flew open so fast that my eyelashes tickled my eyelids.

"Rian," I husked out from a throat unused to speaking for too long.

"I'm here, my love."

Rian's face hovered over mine. Concern etched his dark brows, so at odds with the silvery blond of his hair. Worry pinched the lines of his face.

"What happened?" I lifted my shoulders, but Rian's hands pushed me back onto the mattress.

Mattress? A bed made of twisted tree branches in a four-poster bed surrounded me along with thick navy-blue curtains closing us into an intimate space. The space was gloomy, but not dark, suggesting there was a glow coming into the bedroom from a window or lights, but as I shifted my gaze up, I noted the absence of light fixtures in the ceiling.

"Where am I?" I dropped my gaze back to Rian's face.

A muscle in his jaw ticked. The light in his indigo-rimmed eyes was as dull as our enclosed space.

"Rian?"

He swallowed so hard, his Adam's apple bobbed up and down. A tear fell from his right eye onto his cheek.

Every second that ticked by, my worry grew.

I slid my hands to his chest over the rapid beating of his heart. It pounded so hard, I was afraid there was something wrong with him.

"Hey," I whispered. "Whatever it is, it's all right."

He shook his head, then dropped it to my chest, sliding his arms around my back and hugging me tightly. I wrapped my arms around his back and held on tight to my mate. I'd never seen him so distraught. It made my heart ache.

After a long moment, he rolled off me, cupped my face, and kissed my lips so lightly I almost thought I'd imagined it.

"I almost lost you," he rasped out.

"What are you on about?"

"Don't you remember?"

"What?"

He sat up and slid his hands to the hem of the nightgown covering my body to my feet. I grinned in amusement as he drew the long gown up my body until his fingers brushed my thighs taking all my hilarity away and setting a flame of desire over my nerve endings. He didn't keep touching me though as I hoped. He inched the long nightgown over my legs and waist then touched a tiny pink spot on my side over my ribs and very close to my heart.

"Someone wounded you. Here." He brushed his finger back and forth testing the spot for tenderness. "'Tis almost healed now. That's why you awoke."

"I..." I placed my hand on top of his holding it against my skin.

His palm warmed as his power surged and soaked into my skin as a flare of bronze-gold-colored light emanated from his hands.

"I should have been with you, but I wasn't. This is my fault."

"Rian. No." I frowned trying to find the memory in my mind. I searched back in time recalling our last moment together at the waterfall, going home to the jungle and parting once again, then heading out on a poacher hunt. I sucked in a harsh breath. The attack came screaming back into my mind along with the pain of the gunshot wound and the scent of the gunpowder. Then there was the warm wetness of my blood gushing from my body. "Fuck. They shot me."

"This was a gunshot wound?" Rian smoothed his palm over my side.

"Yes, the fucking poacher shot me." I pushed Rian's hand away and sat up. "I need to get back."

"You'll do no such thing." He rubbed a hand over his crown. "You almost died, and you're not completely healed, otherwise you'd have no scar."

"But my colony? Everyone will wonder where I am."

"Laz told me you were dead. They all believe you're dead. They'd given up on you."

"No. I don't believe that's true." I tugged the nightgown down over my legs feeling exposed and not in a good way. "Laz would have been by my side. He would have known I wasn't dead. Why would he say such a thing?"

"You appeared dead to me when I found you."

"But I wasn't!"

"No, thank Dia, you weren't."

I laid back down, overwhelmed by the notion everyone believed I was dead. The colony... what had happened to them without me?

"Have you been back to Earth? Are the jaguars all right?"

"No. I've been by your side night and day." His hands clenched the bedsheets. "I had more pressing concerns. You jaguars are strong."

I nodded. "Laz would have taken over in my absence."

His lips pulled tight then he said, "I'm sure they're enduring without their queen."

"What if they're not?"

"Then reach for one of their minds. You can still talk to them even when you're here."

"And where's here?"

"My bedchambers in the palace."

"Inside the Summer Court?"

"Aye, where else?"

I rolled my eyes, scooted to the side of the bed, and drew open the velvet curtain. I'd always wanted to see Rian's bedroom for myself and not through his memories. The bedroom was lit with ornate golden twirled candle sconces on the walls. Everyone thought I was dead. What would be the harm in exploring for a short time? Many paintings hung from the walls. I stood and crossed to the closest one, letting my gaze travel over the intricate lines making the flowers in the painting seem real like I could touch their soft petals.

"My youngest sister, Roisin, paints them."

"She's very talented." I moved over to the next one and studied the swirls of the pastel pink paint making the rose bloom. It was magical and captivating.

"Aye, she is." Rian climbed out of the bed and joined me.

A long pair of sleep pants in silky black material covered his lower half but his muscular chest and shoulders were on display. I licked my lips, wanting to trail them over his skin and sink my teeth into his shoulder. Claim him again as my mate. My last thoughts before fading into the darkness came back to me. Wanting to call Rian but not hurt him. Needing him by my side as the feeling left my body but never wanting him to see me die. Pain lanced my heart. If I'd died, he would have lost me, and I would have lost him. Even though our time together was scarce, I always knew he was there for me. What would that feel like if he wasn't? I didn't want to imagine the day of calling to him in my mind and not hearing an answer. He would have experienced that. Been in so much pain. Perhaps more than me while I healed.

I walked around the room to take my mind off what almost happened and focused on the here and now, noting the woven rugs on the floor resembling a field of golden stalks but soft under my bare feet. I dug my toes into the fibers wondering what they used to make the rug. In the center of one wall was an enormous fireplace appearing to not be in use for the lack of ashes. I slipped through a doorway into a bathroom. A large bathtub set on a stand sat beside a window. I leaned over the tub and gazed out the sparkling glass of the window. The view below was astounding. We were high in the palace, many feet in the air, but the tops of golden trees spread for a long distance and beyond the glint of water sparkled. I straightened and made my way out of the bathroom. Rian stood where I'd left him, watching me with a sudden glint in his eyes. I smiled at him, then ducked through the other doorway in the bedroom. On the opposite side was a large sitting room. So enormous, one could dance in it. He'd covered the floor with another rug woven out of golden stalks but this one had purple accents. What plants existed here? From what Rian told me, most of the same plants as on

Earth grew here, but it appeared a few others may exist. Or maybe they'd existed on Earth a long time ago and now no longer did.

I ran a hand over the side table made from light ash-colored wood, and matching chairs made from the same wood, and what appeared like tanned leather, but they must have made it from something else. More paintings of flowers hung on the walls here.

"Very masculine." My lips twitched as I held in my laughter.

"I'll show you masculine." Rian stalked toward me and scooped me up in his arms.

I squealed even as I snuggled into his chest, which I'd been ogling the entire time.

He settled us on one of the inviting-looking chairs. I nibbled his neck with my teeth, giving into my desire. He tugged my hair back.

"Is this your way of telling me you like my bedroom?"

"I like everything about you."

"So, you'll stay?"

I narrowed my eyes. "I didn't say that."

"Sophia." He sighed. "I can't lose you. I almost ended my life when I thought you were dead."

"Rian. No." I cupped his face between my hands. "You must live. So much depends on you."

He rested his forehead against mine. "Nothing more so than you."

"Oh." Was all I managed before I kissed him with all the love I experienced for this Fae prince who was my mate.

He kissed me back so tenderly, he acted like I was fragile. I hissed my displeasure he wasn't being his normal demanding self, but he didn't stop with the gentle kissing. I scraped my nails down his neck. He shivered under my caress. His kiss grew a little more desperate but was still soft. I drew my nails across his chest and circled his nipples. He groaned into my mouth. Slid his hands to my thighs and battled with the length of the nightgown.

I laughed against his lips. He muttered curses against mine.

I drew back. "Did you dress me in this to torment us both?"

"Fae women like long gowns." He caught the hem of the nightgown in his fingers and drew it up my legs once again. "I much prefer your choice of Earth clothes. So much easier access."

"You're a rascal."

"Only for you, my love." He stroked the insides of my thighs, sending flickers of desire straight to my core.

"Please," I scoffed. "As if I believe with your age and skills, I'm— "

He slammed his lips against mine shutting off whatever else I was about to say. His fingers spread my folds, finding me slick with wetness already. He dipped and swirled his fingers teasing my opening and clit in alternating strokes, making me desperate for release. I arched my hips telling him with my body I wanted him inside me to ease this ache he'd built. He lightened his caress, making me more frustrated. I bit his lip, drawing blood and licking it from his mouth. He drew my lip between his teeth and pressed down gradually until my blood burst from a small slice and our blood mingled together. The taste of our blood drove my need for him higher.

His other hand slid up the nightgown and found my nipple. He circled the hard peak until goose bumps pebbled my flesh and made my nipple tight, then he caressed his way over to my other nipple and gave it the same attention. Pleasure shot straight to my core, coating his teasing fingers in a fresh flood of arousal. He slid his fingers into me. I sighed into our bloody kiss, but our skin was already healed and had sealed off the small wounds.

He pumped his fingers as though he was fucking me with them. My need spiraled out of control. Each stroke brought me closer to release. He tugged on my nipples, squeezing them between his thumb and forefinger making my hips buck wildly forcing his fingers into a rhythm of my making. This was what I needed. The hard and fast we were used to. The Rian who took from me while giving me the best sex of my life. Higher and higher my pleasure climbed. Blood roared through my veins and pounded in my ears. Every muscle in my body wound tight. Tighter still as his fingers stroked my sensitive flesh until the pleasure radiated across my entire body as I was lost to the bliss of being with my mate.

My body shattered in a rush as an orgasm exploded from my core. Rian's fingers pushed in deep as I spasmed around them, clenching and releasing them as I would his cock. He crooked his finger inside and stroked a place deep inside that only he could reach. The orgasm rolled on and on. He lightened the tension on my nipple as I sagged in his arms. I gazed up into his face. His eyes blazed back at me as he circled his fingers deep inside me. The relief of the orgasm was gone in an instant as desire flared through me once again.

"I love watching you come. I could spend my entire life like this. Touching you. Pleasuring you. Giving you orgasms until you're supple in my arms."

I wanted to stay with him like this too. A dreamy smile spread my lips. I loved everything about him. The way he gazed at me. Caressed me. Wanted me.

He drew his hands out from under the nightgown leaving me bereft of his touch. A second later, he drew the gown over my head and tossed the garment to the floor. Another second later, he sat me up in his arms and swung my legs on either side of him in the chair. Finally, my bossy Rian was taking control. My body flushed with desire. He tugged his silk pants down enough to free his massive erect cock. Then he lifted my butt with one hand and holding his cock with the other, he lowered me onto him.

We both groaned at the instant mate connection. This here was what it was all about for mates. We stared as my body took his. I raised my hips. Rian cupped my butt cheeks and held me at the tip. Then he lowered me down slowly until I took him in. Up and down, we thrust until the pace grew faster, harder, and more desperate to stay together. My muscles tightened against his cock like a vice not wanting to let him leave. He thrust through the stricture, making my breathing turn ragged and every nerve-ending quivered.

He grabbed my hips and yanked me down hard onto him while thrusting up. That was all it took to send me over the edge into a screaming orgasm. My hips bucked back and forth as my body jerked. Rian's fingers dug into my hips as his release jetted inside me, hitting my sensitive walls, and making my eyes roll back in my head. There was no better feeling than this right here, being one with my mate.

Rian slid his hands up my back, making me shiver. He cupped the back of my head and urged my face to his chest, then he rested his chin on the top of my head. If we stayed like this forever, then I'd be happy. Rian would be happy.

But what about my people?

What about the Fae?

And the plight of both our worlds?

CHAPTER FOURTEEN
RIAN

"**S**AY NOTHING, NOT YET, let me charm you in the way of the Fae before we talk and decide on our future." I stroked her back sending more shivers over her skin.

"For how long?"

"However long it takes. Time moves in a different way here than on Earth."

"How so?" She raised her head.

I shrugged. "It just does. You'll see for yourself. There's no exact equivalent but a day here is but a blip of time on Earth."

She wriggled on my lap. I eased her off my softening cock and stood, drawing her into a stand too.

"Would you like a bath?" I asked.

"Yes, I feel like I haven't bathed for months." She scooped up her discarded nightgown.

"It has been months, my love."

She gasped. "Months here or home?"

"Both."

"So you saying I was here for months could mean I've been gone from Earth for a year?"

"It's hard to say. My mind wasn't on time. I could barely focus to eat let alone think of anything else."

Her face fell. "My people have been all alone for so long."

"They will be fine. You have a well-hidden colony. I've seen the way your soldiers work to protect everyone. I'm sure they would continue to do so in your absence."

"You're right. Laz would have stepped up and taken charge."

A prickle of unease circled the back of my head. When I had the chance, I'd slip back to Earth and check on her people so I could put her mind at rest that they could look after themselves.

"Can you reach out to their minds and check on them?" I asked.

"If I do that, then they'll know I'm alive."

"But you could hear for yourself they are safe."

"True, but I guess if I've been gone months maybe even a year, and everyone thinks I'm dead, then a little more time away won't hurt. A day for me and us before I return home. Is that selfish?"

"Not selfish. You almost died." I ran my hands over her back. "An Earth Day together?"

"I suppose." She frowned.

I grinned. "About a week here then."

"Sneaky." She shook her head. "Bath, then food, I'm ravenous."

"Oh, ah, would you like me to fetch you some meat from Earth?"

"There's no meat here?"

"There is but we don't kill animals to feed from since we're vegetarian and I'm not sure how everyone would react if we started to now." I rubbed the back of my neck.

"It's okay, Rian. I can go a few days without meat so long as there's plenty of carbs like slices of bread and cakes for me to fill up on."

"There are plenty of those. We have superb crops we grind into the best flours. The taste will astound you." I held out my hand. "Come and bathe while I find you clothes."

She slipped her hand into mine. "One of those long Fae gowns hanging to my feet? How will you ever get quick access?"

I laughed. "What you don't realize is Fae don't wear underwear like humans. The access can be just as quick to pull up a long dress as it is to pull off those shorts you're fond of wearing."

"Enough." She dug her nails into my hand, so I'd suffer her jealousy. "I don't want to hear about how you pulled up Fae women's dresses."

"Neither of us was a virgin," I pointed out the truth.

She swung her face to me. "Are you telling me I'll meet your..." She waved her hand. "Fae women?"

"There weren't as many as you imagine." I drew her into my arms. "Not one of them satisfied me in my youth. There weren't any for decades until I found you, so you have nothing to be upset about. The women I was with have long forgotten our dalliance."

"I doubt that very much." She wrapped her arms around my waist. "You're a freaking prince. Any Fae would want to cling to you, let alone any other woman."

"You're putting obstacles in our path that aren't even there."

She laid her head on my chest. "I'm scared, Rian. Give me a moment to process I'm no longer home on Earth, where I've lived all my life. My people think I'm dead and I'm worried about how they all are. Whether more poachers have come and shot them too."

I tipped her chin up. "Reach out to them if you're worried. You can talk into their minds and reassure them you're alive."

"What good would that do?" She pursed her lips. "They'd want me back to lead them as I always have since the queen's role became mine."

"It would reassure you and them you're alive, they're alive, and you can go to them at a moment's notice."

Her dark lashes fluttered against her cheeks as she closed her eyes. Perhaps she wanted this time with me as much as I wanted it with her. If she wasn't reaching out to her people, then there was a reason. I dared to hope I'd convince her to stay here with me. Stay safe in the Summer Court where no poachers could hide in wait to shoot her. Kill her. The rage was back coursing through my body and making my power surge to my hands. She sensed the change in me and drew my hands into hers, watching the swirling bronze-gold colors swirl around our palms.

"I love the touch of your power on my skin."

"You do?"

"Yes, it's warm, and soothing, like your touch, but there's this erotic sensation too."

I rose my eyebrows. "I didn't realize you found my power arousing."

"You're clueless sometimes, mate." She grinned.

"You're not an easy woman to understand, my feisty mate."

"What do you need to know besides bathe me, feed me, pleasure me?" She laughed.

"Hint taken." I led her toward the bathroom.

With a surge of my power, I filled the tub with water and then set flickering orange flames around the edge to heat the water in an instant. I extinguished the flames with a wave of my hand and indicated for her to climb in. She stepped over the lip of the tub and sunk into the water up to her shoulders.

"It's so warm." She sighed.

I lifted a pot of flower petals and sprinkled the pale pink blooms into the bath water. The aroma of rose filtered into the steamy air. Sophia inhaled so deeply her chest rose and pushed the pert tips of her breasts out of the water.

"It's like your paintings have come to life in here." She closed her eyes.

"There's a bar of rose soap on the ledge. Towels are on the hook by the door. I'll be back as soon as I can."

She lifted her hand out of the water and waved me away in a very queen-like manner. I almost laughed at how well she'd slipped into the ways of a Fae royal. She hadn't even glimpsed herself in the mirror and seen her flower crown yet. I wasn't sure how she'd take the addition, but she'd taken my request to stay here for a while easier than I'd believed.

Perhaps I'd underestimated my mate and her need to be with me.

I left her soaking in the large tub even though I'd rather lie in the soothing water with her. There'd be time another day now she was here. My bedroom door clicked shut behind me and I smiled knowing my mate was inside. Alive. Safe. No one would dare hurt a Fae's fated mate inside the Summer Court. Fated mates were sacred no matter what supernatural creature they were. Long ago when we'd lived between the two realms we'd allowed a mixture of mates. Now the Veil locked us in the Summer Court, there were only Fae.

My footsteps echoed down the long marble hallway from my bedchambers into the main part of the palace. Grier walked around the corner leading to the kitchens.

"Your Royal Highness." He dipped a bow.

"Grier, where is Mother?"

She was the only one who knew about Sophia being here and the fact I'd mated with her. She would have discussed my mate with Father by now since it'd been months. They'd left us alone apart from the delivery of food to my door, clean clothes, and books, which had kept my mind occupied while I'd paced the room or laid next to Sophia. I'd forced the food down, but I'd often been unable to eat it all. The stress of my mate lying like death beside me made living unbearable. If she'd died, I wouldn't have survived without her.

"She's in the ladies' waiting room. Shall I fetch her for you?"

"Aye." I nodded my thanks.

He swept away on silent feet, the swish of his red coat the only noise he left in his wake. I sank onto a bench seat feeling older than I ever had. If the spring dried up, would we age at a rapid rate? Would we die within hours, minutes even? The thought made me drop my head into my hands. There was so much to accomplish and yet it all seemed like it was impossible.

"Rian?" Mother's hand touched the top of my head. "She's not...?"

"No." I lifted my head. "She's alive and well."

She set her hands on her chest. "Thank you, Dia. I thought for a second there... What is wrong then?"

"I felt so old suddenly. When the spring stops, I wondered if that was how we would die."

"Oh, sweetheart." She caught my face between her palms. "So much sorrow in your life. I never wished that for you. The spring will renew, wait and see."

"How can you have such faith, Mother?"

"I trust your father. His decisions got us to where we are today, and they'll keep us living. This is what he cares about. Surely you can see that?"

"I do. It's why I've discussed the problem with him and strived to find a solution, but it's critical now. I sense it deep in my power."

"We all do, Rian." She patted my cheeks and let go. "Now, I'll send up the wardrobe I had made for your mate and then we'll see you in the dining hall for dinner."

"You had gowns made for Sophia?"

"Aye."

"She's more of a shorts woman." I laughed at the quizzical expression on Mother's face. "But I'm sure the gowns you requested the seamstresses make will be wonderful."

"Oh, yes, they've used the finest fabrics."

"Of course." I stood. "I should head back upstairs. She'll be wondering where I am."

"I'm so happy she's here, Rian. My son found his fated mate."

"What about Saoirse and her mate?" I frowned, recalling how Father had cast Saoirse out of the Summer Court for finding a fated mate on Earth.

"We'll talk at dinner. There is much to discuss." She strode away, her long indigo gown swishing about her legs with the haste in which she left me staring after her in shock.

Could I hope Father was about to unlock the Veil?

CHAPTER FIFTEEN
SOPHIA

HOW THE WATER STAYED warm this long was beyond me. Fae powers were something to behold, that was for sure. No wonder they'd ruled the Earth. Humans were stupid for thinking they'd take the Fae's power and rule themselves. The Trappers had screwed us all over. Claws sprung from the tips of my fingers as I partially shifted. I would have slaughtered them all like the Fae King and his army.

"Sophia? What's wrong?" Rian asked, hesitating in the doorway.

"I was thinking how stupid humans are. How they put us all in this mess."

"You can't blame them all."

"I know." I sighed and retracted my claws.

"Do you need to shift?"

"No. I'm fine." I stood in the bathtub. "Hand me a towel, please?"

Rian unhooked the plush white towel and draped it around my shoulders. He rubbed my back with the towel, then swooped the great length of my hair up into a tight knot. I stepped out of the tub and collected another towel to dry the rest of my body. Rian observed every tiny movement I made. He almost made me think he was a predator.

"Did you find me any clothes to wear?"

"Mother had gowns made for you. The maids dropped them off."

My eyebrows rose as I wrapped the towel around my body. "Had clothes made? Maids?"

"You're in the Fae palace. What did you think would happen here?"

In the Amazon, I was the Queen, but I was way out of my depth here with the Fae royals.

"I suppose I didn't think about it too much."

He crossed his arms over his chest. "I talked about my home with you."

"You did, and I listened." I stepped closer and placed my hands on his arms. "This—I didn't expect this—grandness and size. You always sounded like you were talking about a cozy house."

He unfolded his arms and took my hands in his. "It is home to me."

"I understand, I do, but give me a bit to take it all in. I'm used to treehouses and caves. Not grand palaces and servants."

"I'll give you everything you want and need."

I smiled. "Right now, I need clothes." My stomach rumbled. "And food."

"This way, my love." He led me into the bedroom.

In the room's corner sat an enormous timber wardrobe with swaths of gowns hanging from coat hangers.

"Dresses?"

"I'll ask the seamstresses to make shorts, but you might need to help them with the pattern. They're only used to making gowns."

"I guess these will have to do for now." I selected an emerald dress. The green gown reminded me of the foliage in my home jungle.

Rian took the towels from my body and returned them to the bathroom. I slid the dress over my head. The fabric was so delicate, my nipples pebbled from the soft caress against my skin. Rian's fingers landed on the back of my collar where he began doing up the multiple buttons down my spine.

"Do you have servants to help you dress too?"

"No. Why do you ask?"

"How would I have done up the buttons without you here?"

He chuckled. His warm breath gusted over my ear and sent shivers down my spine.

"The seamstresses would have expected your mate would help you in and out of the gown."

"Is that right?" I turned around as he fastened the last button.

"And who would have told them I was your mate? You?"

"No. Mother. I was by your side the entire time. I ate in the bed next to you. Stared at you, willing you to wake. The only time I was away from you was to use the bathroom."

His words hit my heart like a sledgehammer with the force of a thousand feelings at once. This Fae prince loved me so much and I'd kept him at a distance our entire time since we'd claimed each other with our mating marks. Well, no more. I stood on my tiptoes and kissed his lips in a fleeting caress.

"Where's my feisty mate gone?" He traced a finger over my lips. "Are you really a sweet... dare I say it?"

"No." I slammed a hand over his mouth knowing too well he was going to say pussycat.

He laughed under my palm. His lips and husky breath tickled my palm.

I narrowed my eyes. "Never call me sweet or I'll use your back for a scratching post."

His laughter grew until I couldn't stand the sensations he was arousing in my body from the mere brush of his lips against my palm. I dropped my hand. He swung the wardrobe door shut. I caught sight of my reflection in the mirror hanging on the wall and gasped.

"Feck," Rian cursed. "I forgot to tell you about your crown."

The shock made me lift a hand to my hair. I hadn't even bothered to wash in the bath because the perfumed flower-scented water was enough to clean what little dirt was there from me lying around for months on end. My fingers shook as I touched a dainty pink flower in my crown. The soft touch of the flower connected to the strands of my hair, then tingled on my scalp and traveled inside my body. I traced a finger over a large blue flower. A spark of electricity shot into my scalp.

"What did you do?" I glared at Rian in the mirror's reflection.

"I saved your life. Gave you a Fae crown as I should have on the day I marked you. This is right, Sophia. It's why the spring healed you."

My mouth fell open as my gaze snagged back on the crown of flowers around my head.

"Your spring healed me?"

"Aye, you're the fated mate of a Fae. You wear the mark of the Fae. This crown is an extension of the Fae royal powers coursing through my body. I made it for you."

My throat constricted as emotion clogged the words in my mouth. I shifted my gaze back to his face. To the indigo-rimmed blue eyes blazing at me with so much love and affection. How could I be angry about this? The crown was beautiful, but it was more. The flowers were a piece of Rian embedded around my head. I should feel like he'd shackled me or marked me in a more obvious way so others would see I was his, but it didn't feel like that was his intention. There was nothing but pure feelings flowing through our mating marks.

"I love you," I whispered inside his head.

"I love you, too," came his immediate reply.

He wrapped his arms around me from behind and rested his chin on top of my head. Our reflections sparkled back at us. His lighter coloring and broad strength enveloped my smaller, lithe frame. I could stay wrapped in his arms forever staring at the love blazing back at me.

"I'm glad you're not angry about the crown."

"For a second I was, but your motives were pure and not masculine bullshit." I smiled.

He tilted his head to the side. "What do you mean?"

"You didn't do it to keep other men away."

His lips spread into a grin. "Perhaps not on purpose, but now that you mention it, I'm sure Laz will hate it."

"What is it with you and Laz?"

"I don't trust him."

"For what reason? Has he given you anything to not trust him for?"

"I don't need a reason other than I am your mate and I can sense his..." He bit his lip. "Never mind about Laz right now. He's not here and my family is. They want us to join them for dinner."

The mention of food made my stomach rumble again. Rian's hand rubbed my flat stomach as though he was trying to soothe it.

"One day, when you're ready, I will love seeing our baby grow here."

"Woah." I placed my hand over his. "How about I meet your family first and stop trying to distract me about Laz? This conversation isn't over."

"Duly noted, mate." He released me from his embrace. "My feisty mate is back."

"You bet your ass she is." I winked. "Don't expect me to act like the princess you've dressed me up to be."

"I wouldn't have you any other way than as you."

"If you weren't such a smooth talker..." I grinned.

"Then what?" he asked when I didn't finish the sentence.

"I don't know," I said half laughing. "I couldn't think of anything."

Rian laughed, and I laughed with him. We were both besotted. In love and happy. He led me out of his room, tucking my arm with his in an old-fashioned way leading me to believe this dinner would be old-fashioned too. I scanned the entire palace as we walked down the marble hallways. It was strange to be wearing this gorgeous gown and be naked underneath. My breasts jiggled with each step, rubbing the delicate fabric against my nipples, and turning them sensitive to the point of torturous arousal. Rian's fingers stroked the inside of my wrist making my pulse burn with need at the slight connection.

Through the long corridors, we turned one way then another. I couldn't recall which way it was back to his bedroom, which was preposterous since I possessed a fantastic sense of direction. If I was ever lost in this gigantic palace, at least I could use my jaguar sense of smell to search out his room if he left me alone. We came to double wooden doors with two servants waiting dressed in deep red attire. They opened the doors before we reached them, and Rian swept us into a grand dining hall.

A long table with enough throne-like chairs to seat dozens of people sat in the center of the room. Orange flames from the candles glowed in the golden candelabras lining the table and highlighting the food. My mouth watered at the delicious scents coming from the table, but I clung to Rian's arm as every person seated at the table stood. All their eyes landed on me. I didn't know where to look or what to say.

"This is my fated mate, Sophia," Rian said.

A pretty blonde woman raced from her chair and hugged me. "I'm Roisin, Rian's youngest sister."

"Oh, you're the exceptional painter."

Roisin blushed. "Thank you."

Another blonde woman came forward, almost identical in appearance to the first. "I'm Ciara." She gave me a quick embrace. "Next youngest."

"Nice to meet you."

An angry-looking woman stood in front of me next. My jaguar instincts reacted, and I curled my lips back in a snarl.

"So, you're a jaguar shifter," she said.

"Aislinn." Rian reprimanded her.

"I bet I could take her," Aislinn said.

Rian opened his mouth, but I placed my finger over his lips, and said, "I'd be happy to test your theory."

A deep masculine laugh exploded behind her, then a man almost identical to Rian pushed Aislinn out of the way. He planted a kiss on my cheek and stepped back with a cheeky wink as I swiped a set of claws at him.

"Feisty." He winked again. "I'm Lorcan. The better brother. Younger, hotter."

I snorted.

Rian laughed. "You're an imbecile."

"Am not," Lorcan said. "I bet if she'd seen me first, she wouldn't be with you."

"Would you two stop?" Briana said coming between her brothers. "I'm Briana. The oldest sister. Wisest too."

"Here we go," Lorcan groaned.

I giggled. I couldn't help it. They were all so powerful, yet so juvenile in the way they acted around each other.

"Nice to meet you, Briana," I said, keeping up the pretense we hadn't met before. Whatever reason Briana had, I wouldn't spill her secrets. These were now my family too.

Rian's siblings returned to their seats. We stepped the short distance to his parents, the King and Queen of the Fae.

"Father, Mother." Rian dipped a bow. "I'd like to introduce you to Sophia."

His mother air kissed both my cheeks. "It's so lovely to meet you."

I eyed the Fae King warily. Would he be as welcoming to me? A jaguar shifter in his Summer Court where he'd locked everyone inside. I must be a big thorn in his side right now with how things had transpired between him and Saoirse now living on Earth with her wolf shifter mate.

The Fae King tipped his chin. "Sophia. Do you have a surname?"

"Moreno." I bobbed my knees in what I thought was a curtsy. *Was I supposed to curtsy? Why didn't Rian give me more of a rundown on the etiquette of the royal court?*

"No need to curtsy, dear," his mother said. "We're all family here."

"Come sit, let's eat. From what my mate tells me, you've been healing for a long time. I remember how hungry Niamh was when she awoke from her long healing," the Fae King said. "She was almost as ravenous when she was pregnant."

His mother giggled in the same way Rian made me giggle. The family resemblance wasn't only in their looks, it was in their personalities too. His mother urged us to sit at the table. The Fae King took his throne-like chair at the head of the table and nodded for us all to sit.

CHAPTER SIXTEEN
RIAN

WHAT THE DIA WAS happening here right now? Why were they all so accepting of my mate? Was I dreaming? Asleep upstairs in bed next to Sophia waiting for her to heal? Or perhaps we were both dead, and this was where we'd ended up?

We passed the platters around the table, everyone muttering their thanks and piling their plates full. I selected a sample of fine slices of bread and roasted vegetables. I surveyed Sophia as she filled her plate with the crusty bread and helpings of legumes seasoned with herbs in an elaborate display on the plate. She'd chosen well to replace her staple of meat with high-protein vegetables. Was it instinct or had she been in this position before? I doubted it. She was too skilled as a huntress. She'd catch whatever she set her mind to.

Before everyone started eating, I cleared my throat. I couldn't take the not knowing any longer.

"I'm sorry, my love, please forgive me for making you wait to eat."

A quiet growl traveled through our mind connection.

"What did I miss these last few months?"

Everyone stared at me, but no one said anything.

"Why are you accepting my mate, not that I'm not grateful, but you didn't accept Saoirse's mate?"

Father shoved back his chair and stood. "Rian, my son, I made a grave mistake with Saoirse. I don't wish to repeat the same mistake with you."

"That's all well and good, but don't you think you should tell her?"

"I intend to."

"How?"

"Rian, so help me." Sophia dug her claws into my arm. "If I don't eat now, then I might just eat you."

Lorcan flipped his head back and laughed.

"Sorry, my love, eat. Everyone, please forgive my interruption to dinner."

Father sat back down and picked up his fork. Sophia dove into her food like she couldn't eat fast enough. I felt like a right shite for making her wait those few more minutes. Whatever I'd missed, and whatever plans Father retained, then I'd find out after dinner. The clink of flatware hit the gold-rimmed plates as everyone dug into their food. A few muttered conversations started between my siblings, but nothing of importance. They talked about the rose garden and Roisin's latest painting. Ciara mentioned she'd found a book about waterfalls and shot me a coy look. I made a note to check in with her later. Lorcan raved about the long line of women trying to convince him to choose them as his mate.

Sophia stopped eating long enough to shoot me a look.

"Mother and Father implored us to choose a mate, so we'd rebuild the Fae, give our people hope too. There have been few fated matings here since Father locked the Veil."

"But to choose a person not fated to you? What would happen if your fated mate came along while you were with your chosen mate?"

"Fate doesn't work like that. Briana chose a mate, and he died at the hand of the Trappers. She met her fated mate the alpha wolf shifter a short time ago."

"So, if Lorcan chose a mate, you're saying fate wouldn't send him his fated one?"

"Correct."

"I don't believe that."

"Have any of you on Earth chosen a mate and then found a fated mate?"

"Well, no, but that doesn't mean..."

"I'm right."

"No need to be so smug."

His deep chuckle vibrated inside my head.

We both glanced at each other and laughed.

"What's so funny?" Lorcan asked.

"Sophia called me smug," I said.

"I didn't hear her talk." Lorcan frowned. "And I'm sitting across from her."

"Jaguar shifters are telepathic. When she claimed me as her mate, she formed a connection between our two minds."

Lorcan leaned across the table. "Well, brother, now I'm jealous. Do you two talk dirty to each other too?"

"Lorcan," Mother scolded.

"What?" Lorcan ducked a cute look at Mother as though he was the sweetest thing since sugar.

"You're all incorrigible." She huffed. "How did I raise such wild offspring?"

"Perhaps you shouldn't have sung at the Water sprite harem balls, Mother," Aislinn said. "Then we wouldn't have all these ideas."

"My singing has nothing to do with this." She huffed.

Father draped an arm around her shoulders and kissed her temple while fighting back a smug grin.

"What am I missing?" Sophia asked.

I turned to my mate. "Mother is a singer. She has an unusual power in her voice. Back before the Trappers ruined everything, she used to travel to Earth and perform at the Water sprite balls. Now, these weren't balls for dancing, although dancing occurred, the dancing was the foreplay. Water sprite balls are notorious for turning into orgies."

Sophia stared at my mother like she couldn't believe the demure Queen had seen such a thing, let alone been on stage to an orgy.

Mother blushed.

Father whispered in her ear, making her blush even harder.

"As I've said over the years, your father was with me every time I went to perform for Sir Axis, and we always left before things got too far advanced."

My brother and sisters laughed. I laughed with them. It was the one thing we'd always embarrassed Mother over and the way Father acted when we did warmed our hearts. He doted on her like she was the most precious being in existence. I glanced at Sophia. I understood how he felt now. A fated mate was the utmost of treasures.

I'd been a fool not to see he'd locked the Veil, so he'd keep his mate safe. I possessed the same sentiments now too after Sophia almost died on Earth.

"Anyway, 'tis rude to not include us in your conversation," Mother said, a teasing glint in her eyes. "Why did you call my son smug, Sophia?"

Sophia lifted her chin and met my mother's smiling face.

"He pointed out fate wouldn't send Lorcan his destined mate if he chose one."

Father cocked his head to the side. "You believed one would find their fated mate while they possessed a chosen mate?"

She shrugged. "I never gave it much thought, to be honest. There are a few jaguar shifters left on Earth, and we tend to stick close together. We're in fact in hiding as are all the supernatural creatures on Earth."

"Hiding? Why?" Father asked.

Sophia placed her flatware on the table. Her plate was almost empty of food anyway, so I said nothing to stop the tirade I sensed coming from her.

"You locked yourselves away in here with no thought to how your absence would affect the rest of us and Earth. From the stories I've been told, after all those burnings and deaths the humans were fearful of anyone with supernatural abilities. They never attacked, but they made living with them in harmony impossible. It became easier for anyone with powers to seclude themselves away from humans. Over time it grew more and more impossible for us to integrate with them."

Father's eyes narrowed to slits as his crown writhed around his head in agitation. "My actions were for the better of my people. What king wouldn't do that?"

"I'm a queen too, you know, and I'd do anything to protect my people but not at the expense of others. There must be a middle ground, otherwise we're selfish."

"How dare you call me selfish," Father bellowed. "I've put everyone's needs before my own time and time again." He slammed his hands on the dining table, his power flared a silver swirl from his hands and twirled up his arms.

Sophia's emerald eyes widened. I placed a calming hand on her arm, touching the soft tufts of her fur and stroking under her skin. She was too close to shifting. Too close to letting her animal instincts take over.

"My love," I soothed as I stroked her arm. "No one could have predicted what would happen."

She flung back her dark hair and turned to me. "This needs to be fixed, Rian. We can't let Earth languish any longer."

"There is something wrong with Earth?" Father asked resuming his seat, the flare in his temper subsiding as fast as it'd come.

"Yes, I sense the change in my jungle which has worsened these last few years."

"What do you mean?" he asked.

"Part of being a jaguar shifter means I can sense vibrations of power and magic. When I'm in jaguar form, I'm connected to the Earth, and the vibrations coming from the magics that make us what we are. They're disjointed. Not vibrating the way they used to. Like the plants and soil used to be in harmony. Now, plant life struggles to flourish. Rain used to fall regularly but now rivers are drying up. It's like the earth is crying in pain."

I stroked a hand through her hair, toying with the flowers of her crown. A tiny shudder ran over her shoulders before she slapped my hand away. Lorcan chuckled across the table from us, so I shot him daggers with my eyes before letting my power flare around his ankles and tying his legs to the chair with a set of vines. I almost made the vines cover his mouth too. Lorcan sat back with a smirk but didn't reveal my childish antics under the table. What was it about my brothers and sisters that made me act so young and impetuous when around them?

"Two realms at odds," Roisin said. "Once they were joined, now they're separate."

We all turned to look at her. For such a young Fae at fifty years old, she possessed wisdom beyond her years.

"The locked Veil is the cause," Lorcan said.

"Let's not jump to conclusions," Mother said.

Father stood. "We shall find out soon enough. Rian, while indisposed with your mate, I arranged for stonemasons to build a tower out in the fields. Inside the tower, I will open a doorway through the locked Veil. I will station guards inside and outside the tower. If by any chance an undesirable comes through the Veil, then we will dispose of them."

I sat back in shock Father had organized such a thing after he'd been so adamant to keep the Veil locked.

"Sounds like a good plan," Sophia said. "A location in the open will afford you excellent protection against anything coming in that you don't want. But I thought only Fae could travel through the Veil?"

"'Tis true, and Fae marked mates," Father said. "My father redesigned the Veil that way after his father's death. Once upon a time, any creature with magic could travel here as they can to the other courts."

"Other courts?" Sophia asked.

"Aye," I said. "There are many realms with many creatures."

"And here I thought Earth housed them all."

I laughed and draped an arm around her shoulders. "You do not know how vast the realms go."

"Why can't we travel to them all?" Her brows puckered in an adorable frown.

"Only special powers can travel between the realms. When we were on Earth there used to be travelers. Most were demons who demanded a cost, who'd transport individuals. I don't know if that still occurs."

She gaped at me like I'd told her the Earth was flat, not round.

I smiled. It was so good having her here in my home sharing my family, and life with her. I should have brought her here sooner. Shown her my world. Other worlds. The entire universe.

"How do these other realms monitor who goes in and who comes out?"

"Guards," Father said. "Like we'll have here. I'm also instating a scribe to document who is traveling in and out. Everyone who leaves will have a guard accompany them."

"For their protection or ours?" I asked.

"Both," Father said.

"Some won't like it."

"They won't have a choice, at least at first. This is the start. If everything goes well, then we'll take the next step to reintegrate back onto Earth. It'll be a long process, so don't expect changes to happen overnight."

"And what about our spring?"

Father frowned. "We'll search for a cure for our spring too. We've almost exhausted our resources inside the Summer Court. It's time to broaden our scope."

I almost asked whether his opening a door in the Veil was more for us to find a cure to our spring than anything else. But whatever Father's motivations, whether it was my mate being here, the spring, the fact Earth was languishing too, Saoirse being on Earth or what, I'd take this step forward and go with it.

The servants cleared the plates and carried out platters with sweet, scented cakes and fruits. Sophia observed them as any predator would a new person in their vicinity, but there was also a little unease in her expression. Being waited on must be an experience for her. One I hope she enjoyed.

We passed around the platters until we'd overfilled our plates with food once again. Sophia devoured the sweet treats like she hadn't already eaten. Crumbs fell onto the top of her dress from the cake in her hand making me want to nibble the sweets from her chest. She peeked at me from under her lashes as though she'd caught my thoughts and gave me a saucy wink.

I cleared my throat. "If you'll excuse us, I'd like to show Sophia around the palace."

Everyone stood, chairs scraping on the stone floors along with mine in my haste to get my mate alone.

"Rian." Father halted us. "Stay inside the palace for now. I have a special plan to introduce your mate to the kingdom."

A trickle of unease ran up my back.

Mother clapped her hands in excitement. "We're holding a ball."

My brother and sisters groaned. I fought back a groan of my own.

"A ball?" I queried.

"Aye." Mother beamed. "The seamstresses are making us all new attire. We'll present your father's plans to the people and introduce your mate. It'll give them hope they too might find a fated mate on Earth."

"After we present your mate to the kingdom, you can take her on a tour of the Summer Court," Father said.

Sophia slid her hand into mine and dug her nails into the back of my hand. Guess my mate was a little unsure of a ball. I'd have to ask her if she knew how to dance. I doubted a jaguar shifter living in the wilds of the Amazon learned ballroom dancing, but I looked forward to teaching her.

CHAPTER SEVENTEEN
SOPHIA

I CLUTCHED RIAN'S ARM as he led me out of the dining hall. Any minute now I'd shred the sleeve of his jacket, but he didn't seem to mind the flickering of my jaguar shape dancing under my skin.

Dancing.

I broke out into a cold sweat.

"I can't dance," I whispered.

Rian gazed down at me with such affection I couldn't help feeling the love flowing between us.

"I wondered if you'd say that." He stroked the sensitive skin on the inside of my wrist.

My nerves fluttered and then settled with his calming touch. Why could my mate put me so at ease when I was so out of sorts?

"Don't worry, I'll teach you tonight under the moonlit sky. I know the place no one will see you stepping on my toes."

"Hey." I squeezed his arm.

He chuckled. "I'm sure my feet can handle your tiny bruises."

I rolled my eyes. "Stop teasing. This is serious. It sounds like this ball is a big deal, so I need to be... well, what's the word I'm looking for?"

"Royalty?"

"Maybe."

"You are royalty. Not only are you a queen of your people but you're a Fae princess now. Double the dose. You can't get more royal than you," Rian said as he led me through the maze of marble hallways.

"Where are we going?"

"First, I want to show you the spring."

"I am intrigued by this spring. You Fae hinge a lot on it."

"Aye, 'tis important to us our Spring of Life, giver of immortality, healer of grievous injuries. It's where you healed after all."

We walked through the doorway into an atrium. The scene made me gasp. Crystal-clear water flowed over a rock face into a pool beneath. Smooth pebbles glinted under the moonlight coming in through the open roof of the room and giving the water a magical glow. On the edges of the ceiling hung an array of flowering blooms draping down as though they were reaching for me. I lifted a hand and touched a soft white blossom, releasing even more of the fragrant scent into the surrounding air. Tiny glowing lights floated in the air, buzzed around our faces then floated back up into the sky.

"It's magical, Rian." I spun around to take in the wonder of the place. "I understand why you covet it so."

Rian caught my waist in his large palms and halted my spinning.

"I covet you." He wet his lips. "Nothing compares to you."

"You're such a sweet talker. It's no wonder you've got me wrapped around your little finger." I licked my lips.

"'Tis the other way around, my love."

"Shut up and kiss me."

Rian obliged my demand. His firm lips landed on mine in a ravenous kiss that also worshipped me. Told me how much he hungered for me with the swipe of his tongue against mine until I moaned into his mouth and tugged at his jacket trying to get to the man underneath all the fancy clothes. Rian caught my hands in his and ended our kiss.

"Dance lesson first."

I pouted.

He kissed my pout, then nipped my bottom lip with his teeth.

"Here?" I asked. While the space was large enough, they'd made the floor of cobblestones and I was sure would make me trip more than anything else.

"No. A place you'll love. Trust me." He wrapped his hand around mine and led me out of the atrium.

We weaved through more marble hallways until we walked under large golden arches onto a smooth floor.

"What is this place?"

"This is where we spar."

I raised my eyebrows, taking in the place's expanse with a view of how one would fight in the courtyard. The area was open, with no cover to be found. This was a place to pit skills not to fight.

"You train here?"

"Aye. With our powers, swords, staffs, daggers. You name it, we've trained with it."

"What about jaguars?" I slashed my claws in the air.

He laughed. "No, no jaguars or other shape shifters. Fae only."

"I only know how to fight as a jaguar, or with fists and feet like a human. And how to shoot a gun, though I prefer to stay away from them." My hand slid to my side, touching the now-healed wound, but my mind recalled the burn of the bullet digging into my flesh.

"With good reason." He firmed his lips.

I cracked my knuckles. "I'd like to try this place out."

"We will. Dancing."

"That's not what I meant, and you know it."

"I'm not fighting my mate." He folded his arms.

I tapped my foot. "Come on, it'll be fun."

"Fun for who?" His left eyebrow rose.

"Fun for me," Aislinn said, strolling into the area as though she owned it.

I stood up straight. This was the hostile sister. What had I ever done to her? My jaguar shape hummed under my skin, ready to take her on if she took one wrong step toward me or Rian.

"You fight too much." Rian turned to his sister.

"We have a lot to fight for." She peered from her brother to me. "So, are you two going to fight or shall we give it a go?"

I grinned in a bloodthirsty way, showing her my pointed teeth a split second before I threw a punch at her face and landed the blow on her lip, making it split open and spill blood. My jaguar side inhaled the metallic scent of blood with triumph.

"You're fast," Aislinn said.

"She is," Rian said. "So help me, Aislinn, if you hurt my mate..."

"We're playing, isn't that right, Sophia?"

"Yes, we're playing. We won't hurt each other."

We both looked at each other and said, "Much."

I swiped a leg at Aislinn's. She anticipated the move and jumped in the air missing my strike with more ease than I'd expected after I'd landed the first blow. Her fist flew toward my face. I ducked and missed the blow. I swung toward her stomach, but she scooted back. She spun in the air with a kick aimed at my face I saw coming a mile away, so I avoided that too. As our trades in blows went on, neither of us landed a single hit.

Aislinn and I stopped for a split second to resize our opponent. She was as fast as me, but she was holding back her Fae power and if she brought that out, then I'd have to bring out my jaguar shape.

"All right." Aislinn lowered her fists. "I accept you're a good fighter."

"You're pretty good yourself." I lowered my hands to my sides. "It's hard fighting in these dresses." I yanked at the long material of the dress.

Aislinn smiled the first genuine smile I'd seen on her face. "They are cumbersome. I prefer pants myself, but us royals must keep up appearances."

"In what way?" I smoothed back my damp hair from my face, catching a finger on a flower in my crown that I'd forgotten was there until the touch sent a weird sensation through me.

"Familiarity comforts our subjects. They like seeing us in pretty dresses looking sweet and demure." She curled her top lip. "We're anything but, yet..." She waved her hand up and down the gown on her body. "Looks are deceiving. No?"

I stopped messing with my hair and eyed his sister. She was the pretty picture of a Fae princess dressed in a delicate lilac gown, her long blonde hair braided into an intricate curl around her head. While it appeared she'd braided her hair to look elegant, I now grasped she tied the long strands back so it wouldn't impede her fighting. She was a warrior under the disguise of a pretty princess. I slid my gaze to Rian. Under his regal appearance, he was a warrior too.

"Yes, we can use looks like camouflage. I can sneak up on my enemy and I bet you can too."

Aislinn reached for her ankle and drew a dagger out from under her long dress.

"Sneak up, slide this into their heart, and be gone before they even feel the blade or hit the ground."

I stopped myself from shuddering at the brutal glint in her eyes.

"Aislinn." Rian placed his hand over the top of the blade. "Your enemy is dead. Father killed all the Trappers."

Aislinn lowered her arm and shoved the knife back into the holster around her ankle. "Don't be a fool. Enemies will always be." She stomped off before I agreed with her.

"Sorry about my sister," Rian said, shaking his head after her retreating back. "The Trappers captured her. They tied her to a stake and set her on fire before Lorcan rescued her. To say it affected her would be an understatement."

I tapped the side of my head. "I recall your memory of the night she returned. Ash and soot covered her, and they'd burned her feet, but they didn't injure her gravely like your mother."

"No, she wasn't, but she's been bitter since then."

"It was hard for you all." I stepped into Rian's body and wrapped my arms around his waist.

He returned my embrace. "I will not lie. What was hard was watching you spar with my sister."

"It was fun." I giggled. "She's a good fighter. Do you think she accepts me now?"

"She accepted you before. Otherwise, she would have buried the dagger in your heart like she's capable of doing."

I tipped my chin up to meet his amused expression.

"You're such a tease." I wriggled my body against his. "I'm all sweaty. Let's head back to your room."

His hands cupped my buttocks and stilled my squirming hips. "Stop trying to get out of dance lessons." I groaned.

He lifted one of my hands and placed it on his shoulder, cupped my hand in his, and lifted them in the air. His other hand slid to my waist. A breeze blew in through the open ceiling of the courtyard sending a cool caress over my heated skin.

"Be glad we get to dance this close these days. In medieval times, the couples only touched hands as they pivoted around each other." He drew my hips against his. "Now I can hold you close and guide you into the steps."

I licked my lips as a telling twitch in his pants made instant desire light a path through my body.

"I think this is a ploy to feel me up in front of everyone."

He threw his head back and laughed. Such a joyous sound. A thrill ran through me I'd given him such pleasure.

I batted my eyelashes. "Not that you need a ploy." I leaned in close to his ear. "You can feel me up anytime."

He pressed the side of his cheek against mine. "Oh, I will. But for now, dance, my love. Think of it as sparring. One step forward, two steps back."

His feet moved and mine followed along with his as he hummed a song under his breath. A quiet tune holding a note of seduction. I fell under his spell, letting him lead me around the courtyard, our bodies finding the natural rhythm. Two halves, one whole. Fated mates were made for each other.

The silvery streams of moonlight sparkled on the floor, the walls, and over the golden archways giving the space a magical sensation and sending a hum through my body. Rian moved with such ease that it was obvious to see this was where he was at home. In this palace. In this realm. A Fae prince who lured me to love him, even more, each moment we spent here.

I'd been selfish wanting him to spend our time apart. To be two royals in two different places. We were no longer those things. Rian and I were joined. We'd marked each other ten years ago. It was time we were together as fate intended. I'd told him to give me time, but I think I'd already decided to stay in the Summer Court with him.

"You're doing so well." He spun us in a circle and waltzed us back to the other side of the courtyard.

"I've only stepped on your toes a few times."

I cursed my stupid gloating as I stepped on his foot again. Rian chuckled. Then hummed a new tune.

"Sounds pretty." I sighed. "Does the song have words?"

"Aye, I'm no singer like my mother but I can sing them to you if you'd like?"

"Yes."

My bonny lass,
She comes a calling,
Her sweet scent luring.
My bonny lass,

She comes to me,
Her sweet delights tempting.
My bonny lass,
She comes for me,
Her sweet juices...

"Rian." I slapped my hand on his shoulder. "Those are surely not the words to the song."

His eyes sparkled as he laughed. "No, they're not. I can't take a second longer of holding you in my arms and not tasting you."

"Good. Let's go."

"Go where?" He kneaded the cheeks of my buttocks while inching the skirts on my dress up. "You said you wanted me to show you how easy I could get to you in this dress."

"But..." I peered at the archways to the courtyard. "Anyone can walk in. There are no doors."

"And?" The skirts reached the tops of my thighs, and he slid his fingers to the bare skin of my butt, needing and stroking the flesh until I couldn't think straight. He backed me up against a wall. His fingers slid to the front finding me damp with arousal already. He stared at my face as he slid two fingers deep inside me. "Do you want me to stop?"

"No." I arched my hips, urging him to keep playing with my eager flesh.

He leaned forward and ran his tongue up my neck. "Mmm, sweet and salty." He dropped to his knees, buried his face between my thighs, and swiped his tongue over my clit.

"Rian," I moaned.

The sound was quiet, but my nerves prickled. Someone could hear me. I bit my lip. Rian circled his tongue over my clit while his fingers pumped inside me. Soon my mind was blank to the building tension in my body. My thighs quivered, but Rian used his shoulders to keep me upright and spread open. This whole no underwear thing was good. Why did I question it?

My head fell back against the wall as my toes curled and I lifted higher to Rian's fast fingers pounding into me. He yanked me back down by the hips with his other hand forcing my clit into the suction of his mouth and stroking me so deep, stars blinked into existence in my vision. Watching my mate feast on me like a ravenous beast was so freaking hot. I couldn't take the pleasure anymore. I shattered into a thousand starlit pieces as my orgasm burst free shaking my legs and body in the pleasure's rapture.

Rian suckled my orgasm into his mouth, moaning the entire time like he was enjoying every second his tongue lapped at my juices. He stood in a rush, yanked his pants down far enough so his massive, hard cock sprang free, and he impaled me against the wall.

"Couldn't wait any longer," he rasped out between thrusts.

I licked my juices from his jaw and devoured his mouth in a kiss letting him know I didn't care. I wanted him like this. My wild, sexy Fae prince was out of control when he had to have me. He picked my legs up and hooked them around his waist giving him deeper access. I clung onto him as he thrust into me with furious strokes sending my sensitive flesh back into a fever pitch of tension.

Then he did something he'd never done before.

His power coated his fingers. My skin exploded like a live wire of electricity. He slid his hands between us, spread my lips, and gave a long slow thrust, pausing while buried deep inside me, he swiped his thumbs over the side of my clit.

"Don't stop," I gasped out through the height of ecstasy racing through my body as my core clamped down on him holding him in deep and not wanting to let him go.

He drew his cock out to the tip and eased back in again all the while brushing his power over my clit. The pleasure was too much. My vision darkened. Rian brought me higher to the peak of pleasure with each glide of his cock, each caress of his power. It was like he claimed every part of me once again. As he thrust again, the ripples of my orgasm started before he'd even buried himself deep. Each slight slide of his cock made the orgasm ripple harder until he seated himself fully and came with me. Our bodies rolled together on the euphoric waves of bliss. Of stars and moonlight. Of mates and love.

I'd never been more at home than right here, with Rian.

What did that say for my people back on Earth?

Tears welled in my eyes and trickled down my cheeks. Rian brushed them away and cupped my cheeks in his warm palms still glowing a bronze-gold of colors with his power.

"What's wrong, my love?"

"I want to stay with you." I swallowed through the thick emotion in my throat. "This place is so magical. It's woven threads around my heart and tied me in place. I've never been happier than here with you."

He eased out of me and smoothed the skirts of my dress down my legs before tucking himself back into his pants.

"Why so sad then?"

"I'm neglecting my duty. Ignoring my people. Everything I've fought so hard for to keep them alive has been like living in hell and now I'm in heaven. The guilt of leaving them is churning my stomach. How could I do that? Even think it?"

"Whatever you decide, I'll be your mate forever."

"That's another problem. I feel like it's my fault we weren't together the last ten years, and I robbed us of this happiness."

"Never your fault. We both made choices. We discussed it all rationally."

"I love you, I do, and I should have put this mate bond first."

"As should have I." He lifted me into his arms.

"Rian, put me down."

"No." He sat us on the floor and cuddled me to his chest. "My mate is upset, and I'll cuddle her until she's not."

I buried my head into his chest. "Never let me go."

"Never. I'll be with you wherever you go."

"Promise?"

"Aye. From dawn to dusk. You'll be very tired of me soon."

I smiled into the fabric of his coat. "I doubt that but what if you tire of me?"

"Not a chance in any realm." He stroked my hair over my shoulder.

"I'll need to head home and make sure everyone is safe and Laz is doing his duty before I can live here permanently."

"Of course. I'll accompany you whenever you're ready."

"I may never be ready, but after being stuck in the palace and then a ball, can you show me the rest of the Summer Court first?"

"I'm looking forward to it."

CHAPTER EIGHTEEN
RIAN

THE DAYS IN THE Summer Court were the best time of my life. Waking to my mate and devouring her in my bed, making her scream loud enough the walls almost shuddered. We'd bathed together, wandered the great hallways together, and snooped in every room like a pair of lovesick youths sneaking kisses and caresses everywhere. We'd crossed paths with all my family members and Sophia had taken the time to get to know them all a fraction more. She'd sparred with Aislinn. Whispered to Briana. Admired Roisin's paintings. Read the books Ciara recommended about the Fae. She even put up with Lorcan's lame attempts at flirting with her. We'd spent a few afternoons drinking sweet berry tea with Mother and Father in the sunroom. They'd tried hard to treat Sophia as though she was one of us. Sophia even talked to the servants and asked them their names. We'd dined with the family every night, then I'd taken her to the courtyard for more dance lessons. She'd almost perfected her dance steps, but when she was in my arms, I didn't care if she stepped on my toes from time to time.

As I dressed for the ball in the dark green suit embroidered with gold stitched leaves and the occasional dainty white flower, I gazed at Sophia. She wound her hair into a curl at the back of her neck. She'd yet to dress and stood naked and beautiful in my bedroom tempting me to forgo the ball and have my way with her yet again.

I'd never tire of her.

She caught me looking and winked.

I smiled, licked my lips, and finished sliding the emerald buttons into place at the sleeves of my jacket. "As beautiful as you are naked, I can't very well dance with you at the ball like this."

She grinned in her mischievous, sexy way. "I'm sure you can."

"Aye, I could, but I would be most uncomfortable wanting to fuck you into oblivion and gouge out the eyes of every man who saw you."

Sophia laughed, deep and husky like a taunt to my already inflamed desires.

"Nudity doesn't bother shifters." She stroked a hand over the curve of her breast and down the tight muscles of her stomach.

I caught her hand in mine and kissed her palm. "Stop delaying the inevitable."

"Do I have to go?" She pouted.

"Aye." I spun her around and swatted her butt.

"Hey." She angled her chin over her shoulder and sought to look upset but failed.

"Dress now, please, my love."

"Fine." She huffed and collected the deep green gown from the coat hanger.

She stepped into the long skirts and pulled the material up to her waist, then slid her arms into the sleeves and up over her shoulders. With her body now out of sight but not out of my mind, I admired the fall of the dress on her lithe frame. The material clung around her form like a second skin, almost like her jaguar shape. The green of the material matched mine, as did the embroidery of flowers and leaves except her gown held an abundance of tiny white flowers across the bust and along her waist until they spread out in a spattered array over the skirts of the dress.

"Can you tie the back please?" She turned around giving me a view of her slender back and the ribbons of the corset-style design.

I inched closer and tugged the silky ribbons tight across her back piece by piece. Satisfied I'd neither tied the corset too tight nor too loose, I tied the ribbons into a bow and kissed the back of her bare shoulder.

"You look divine." I faced her toward the mirror.

Her eyes skated over our reflection, up and down. She kept looking at every tiny piece of the outfit as though something new popped out at her each time.

"When I was the Queen of the Jungle..."

"You still are."

Her lips pulled down. "Maybe. Who knows what's happening in the jungle."

"Have you reached out to any of your people?"

"No." She shook her head. "I'm being selfish, I know I should, but..."

"'Tis not selfish to put yourself first for once in how many years?"

"Oh, Rian." She spun around and clasped the sleeves of my jacket. "It is, but right now I don't care about anything but you. Soon we'll go back together and see my people are fine without me."

"We will," I said because she would always be a queen and I'd always support her, but I grinned with happiness because all I'd ever wanted was to have her choose me. Her fated mate. I stroked my knuckles over her cheek. "I'm happy you're here."

"Me too," she whispered.

"Come, let's do this big reveal Father has planned, then I can hold you in my arms and dance with you all night."

She slid her arm through mine. "Do you think it'll be that easy?"

"No." I chuckled.

She pinched my arm, and I laughed harder as I led her out of my bedroom and through the long, winding hallways toward the grand ballroom. We hadn't used the room in a long time. Things were changing for the better I hoped. The King and Queen hosting balls again would make our people happy. They'd always enjoyed singing, dancing, feasting, and drinking. The Summer Court had been a happy place until recent times.

Grier rushed up to us, his red coat jacket flying like wings in his haste. "Your Royal Highness." He dipped a bow. "Her Royal Highness." He bowed at Sophia too.

A tiny flare of red seared her cheeks. Being royalty here was a lot different from the wilds of the Amazon.

"If you'll please come with me. Your Majesty has asked I bring you to the back of the stage where he can present you both in a flourish."

"Very well," I said.

I smirked. Trust Father to cut off any rumors before they'd even started. If Sophia and I wandered around in the ballroom before anyone learned about Father creating a doorway through the locked Veil, then they'd question her presence. He'd thought everything through to perfection. This way there was a reason Sophia was here. This way it would appear he'd sent me to Earth, and I hadn't done so behind his back. It would show his strength to be absolute still. He was a brilliant king even if he made mistakes.

We followed Grier to a back door of the ballroom. He led us into the enclosed space behind the stage, beyond came the sound of the musicians playing their instruments, and beyond that was the chatter of the Fae congregated inside. Sophia scanned the gloomy space, her keen gaze noting escape routes. She was a superb queen too, and an even better predator, plus she knew how to survey an area for threats in a minute amount of time. After a short time, she relaxed. I nodded at a row of chairs set up for the performers to rest, which were still vacant. Father would have kept them out of here too, so Sophia's presence wasn't revealed too soon. She shook her head and shifted from foot to foot. If I didn't know better, I'd say she was about to fight or run.

Perhaps she was.

The music stopped. A hush descended over the ballroom with an expectant air. I almost sensed the thrum of excitement coming from every Fae inside. Father's voice boomed from the stage. Every word was clear as though we stood beside him. As he spoke each word, each sentence about the Veil and the door he'd created, a ripple of voices began in the ballroom. Until he silenced them all with a command and a surge of his King's power.

"I understand you all have questions," the King said. "As this is new to me too, then I might not have the answers yet, but I will do everything in my power to get those answers."

"Will we be safe on Earth?" a man yelled.

"I will endeavor to see to your safety as I always have, but I cannot guarantee your safety on Earth." He paused. "Earth has changed since we last frequented the realm. While there are no Trappers left in existence... there are different dangers."

"What dangers?" the same man yelled.

Beside me, Sophia's fur brushed under her skin against my hand on her arm.

"I'm unaware at this stage of the dangers, but my son Rian has traveled to Earth through the new door and returned unharmed. He found his fated mate on Earth."

A collective gasp echoed through the ballroom. The people's voices grew louder as their whispers became enthusiastic words.

"Why are they so excited?" Sophia asked.

"We haven't had a fated mating here in centuries. Some believe it's why we've had so many problems with our birthrate."

"Let me introduce you to Princess Sophia Moreno. Rian's fated mate," the King bellowed.

"That's our cue." Sophia plastered on a fake smile covering the sadness she'd exhibited on her face moments before.

"Aye." I led her up the staircase.

Thick burgundy curtains hung from the side of the stage, and for an extra moment, they covered us in darkness before we stepped onto the stage. Mother and Father stood in the center awaiting our entrance. We made our way over to them, Sophia clung to my arm the entire time, but she was careful not to dig her claws into the fine material of my jacket. We turned and faced the crowd.

Every eager Fae face in the room followed our movement. Mouths hung open in shock. It was clear for all to see Sophia wasn't a Fae, but then again, we had no reason to believe we left any Fae on Earth. For our people to hear and see I possessed a fated mate must be a surprise. One I'd kept hidden for ten years. Now I didn't have to. I was proud to have Sophia on my arm as my mate. Fated mate no less. This moment here was a huge beacon of hope for all our futures.

"Welcome," I called out to the crowd. "This is my fated mate, Sophia."

"What is she?" a woman yelled.

Sophia squared her shoulders. "I'm a jaguar shifter."

The murmurs were back in the crowd.

"'Tis no matter what she is. All that concerns anyone is she's my fated mate."

A chorus of "Ayes," ran through the crowd. Then they applauded. I held Sophia's hand up in mine high in the air and brought it to my lips. The crowd clapped louder.

"Mother, would you please sing us a song?"

"It would be my honor, my son." Mother beamed.

Father descended the stairs to the goldstone ballroom floor. I led Sophia down the stairs, keeping her hand in mine. Back up on the stage, the musicians plucked a tune. The crowd spread as we made our way into the center of the dancefloor. Up above the candles in the golden chandeliers burst into a brighter flare of light. I gathered Sophia into my arms. She tipped her chin up at me, the feisty streak still there even as she trembled.

Mother's voice soared out into the ballroom coating every Fae with the magic in her singing. It was my turn to make certain they accepted Sophia, and she would be once Mother used the unusual power in her voice in this song.

Through the Veil,

A meeting was fated.
Under the sky,
A prince wandered lost.
In the jungle,
A jaguar stalked her prey.
Trees trembled with hope,
Clouds cried with joy,
The sun beamed with happiness.
And two hearts searched for one.
Over the Veil,
Their meeting was destined.
Above the soil,
The prince found focus.
In the darkness,
The jaguar tracked love.
Leaves embraced their union.
The river glistened with tears.
Birds sang their pleasure.
For two were fated to become one.
Two hearts beat together.
Fated mates forever.
Their love knows no bounds.
Fated mates forever.
Ever.
And.
Ever.

With each word Mother sang, I caressed the back of Sophia's waist in a soothing embrace to each dance step. Mother's words rippled across the expanse of the ballroom, filling each of us with a sense of belonging and happiness for a fated mate. We all held that belief anyway, but she'd solidified the sentiment with her powers.

Not one person danced with us. They watched, soaking in our connection like it was magic itself. Perhaps they'd covet what we possessed, but they'd never go against a fated mating. We may be powerful Fae but even we deferred to fate. Sophia's trembling stopped as she glided across the floor with me. Her feet didn't miss a step as she let me lead her. Her hips swayed in time to mine in a sensual dance of lovers who appreciated each other's bodies.

I dipped my mouth to her ear and nibbled on her earlobe pretending I was whispering in her ear.

"Behave," she whispered into my mind.

"I cannot help myself when I'm with you."

"Every eye is on us."

"So?"

"I don't wish for you to gouge out all their eyes tonight."

Her face spread into a grin as she shifted her ear out of my reach.

"I quite like this dress and don't want blood on it."

I chuckled and pressed her closer as Mother broke out into a new song.

"She's a phenomenal singer," Sophia said.

"She is," I agreed.

"Will they all stop looking at me soon?" She peeked over my shoulder at the crowd still staring at her in obvious interest.

"Who knows? You are way too beautiful to stop looking at."

She shook her head. "Sweet talker."

CHAPTER NINETEEN
SOPHIA

T HE FAE BALL WAS even more special than the ones
I'd seen in Rian's memories. Experiencing the
Summer Court in person was a whole other world.
One that made me feel welcomed. No poachers were
hunting the jaguars here. The Summer Court was safe.
No wonder the Fae King fought to keep the Veil locked.
Feeling safe for the first time in my life was like a huge
lift of pressure from my very shoulders.

But the nagging sensation I should check on my
colony sunk into my skull and gnawed a hole in my
happiness.

Rian was attentive as always, and he didn't leave my
side. He danced with me and doted on me. Introduced
me to people who gaped at me with equal parts awe
and flickers of desire flashing in their eyes. They weren't
malicious though. The Fae people weren't anything but
the best hosts. They lay trays of food out on a long table,
and we helped ourselves when we needed a moment

alone. Rian filled my plate with small parcels of sweet delights that melted in my mouth, but the food didn't stop me from craving meat.

It was the only thing that would make this place perfect. I wouldn't survive here forever without the substance of meat. The jaguar part of me needed it. Longed for it. Before too long, I wouldn't be able to keep my jaguar inside and I'd go hunting for fresh meat myself. I peeped at the Fae from under my eyelashes. Would I horrify the Fae if I stalked their wildlife? Traumatize them if I devoured an animal in front of them?

I took the sparkling crystal goblet Rian held out to me. A deep burgundy liquid sloshed in the crystal as I brought it up to my lips. Warmth slid down my throat as I drank half the goblet in one mouthful.

Rian rose an eyebrow in question, but another over-welcoming Fae came forward, gushing over how lucky we were. How she couldn't wait for the next Fae royal to be born, so we'd celebrate even more. I bristled beside Rian. This was the second time there'd been mention of a baby. In the ten years we'd mated, neither of us mentioned conceiving a child. I almost tasted the desperation of the people for a more auspicious sign of their future.

And it all seemed like it hinged on me.

The pressure in the room weighed me down. Rian detected my sagging demeanor.

He leaned into my ear and whispered, "Have you had enough?"

"Yes," I whispered back.

"Excuse us," Rian said, sweeping me away from the lady and toward his parents. "Mother, Father, we are retiring for the night. Thank you for your grand gesture. My mate and I appreciate it."

Mother kissed my cheeks, then Sophia's. Father nodded his head, his gaze always assessing the situation and people.

"Good night," I said. "Thank you for the welcome party."

Rian strode from the ballroom with my arm linked with his, our heads high even as we sensed the curious expressions of everyone watching us leave. Out in the quiet hallway, I snuggled under Rian's powerful arm. He placed it around my shoulders, drawing me in even closer as we made our way back to his bedroom. I yawned long and loud.

"What time is it?" I asked.

"Late. The moon is lowering to the horizon. Dawn will be upon us soon."

"No wonder I'm tired." I stifled another yawn.

"Too tired for me to claim you in this gown?" Rian asked as he swung open his bedroom door.

I swept into the room. "I'm never too tired for you."

Rian locked the door, strode toward me, and lifted me by the waist to toss me on his bed. I landed with a puff of air exploding from my lungs and the fabric of the skirts flying around me. He stalked me, more predator than me at this moment. I opened my arms and legs as he climbed onto the bed. As good as the night had been, ending it in the arms of my fated mate was even better.

The sun was well and truly in the sky before we awoke. A servant left a breakfast tray outside Rian's door, so we ate brunch in his bed before dressing and heading outside the palace walls. Rian walked me through the rose garden at the back of the palace, the array of perfumed blooms swayed in the gentle breeze. Each petal appeared like a piece of velvet. I stroked a finger over a deep pink bloom as we left the rose garden and walked into the forest beyond. Giant trees with golden leaves aglow like living flames of sunlight stretched to the blue sky. Their silvery white bark added to the magic of the forest. So different from the greens of the jungle I'd lived in.

We skirted the edge of the lake next. The enormous expanse of water sparkled under the sun, but even to me a new visitor, I could tell the lake had decreased as the shore was larger than it should have been. Although the gentle laps of the water on the soil were soothing.

"Are they the giant lily pads I spotted in your memories?" I pointed into the distance across the surface of the lake.

"Aye. We can swim out to them if you'd like?"

"Not today." I shook my head.

"You've been very quiet today," Rian noted.

"It was a long night."

"Hmm."

"Where to next?"

"If you're tired, we can nap."

I swept my hair back over my shoulders. "I want to keep exploring. It's so different seeing this place in person to your memories."

"Very well." He led me away from the lake and down a long dirt path.

After a short walk, we arrived at the village. Quaint houses lined the cobblestone streets. They'd made their roofs from a straw-colored thatch golden like the rays of the sun while they'd made their walls from a stone that shimmered in the sunlight.

"Is everything always so pretty here?"

Rian smiled. "I've never considered it, but I suppose so."

The Fae greeted us as His Highness and Her Highness as we wandered around the town looking in the windows of the quaint shops.

"Do you pay for these things with money?"

"No." He frowned. "We have no monetary system here. Fae are always willing to give their wares away. No one goes without here."

"Humans use money, so we had no choice on Earth." I pressed a palm to the windowpane and peered at the small carved wooden figurines inside.

"Would you like one?" Rian nodded at the figurines.

"Oh, no. What would I do with a trinket?"

Rian drew me inside the shop. "You'd place it on a shelf, or desk, and remember this day together."

"His Highness, Her Highness," greeted the Fae male inside the shop.

"My mate would like one of your figurines."

"Help yourself."

"Wait," I said. "I can't just take it."

"It would give me great pleasure if you did," he said, tucking the long tails of his shirt into his waistband and smoothing back his hair. "What about this one?" He held up a carved horse.

I shook my head.

"Perhaps this one?" He held up a lion.

"No." I laughed and turned to study the shelf with the figurines.

Each tiny piece of whittled wood hummed with power.

"Did you make these with your power?"

"Aye," he said.

"They're marvelous."

"Thank you." He blushed a deep red.

I spotted a piece of wood carved into the shape of a tree. Straight away the statue drew me to it, and I picked up the tree to examine the carving closer.

"Perfect choice, Your Highness," he said.

"Thank you for your gift." I nodded my head.

"'Tis no gift." He frowned. "It just is."

Rian led me out of the shop, and along another track. This one led to a field of golden stalks blowing in the soft breeze making them rustle and almost sound like they were talking to us. I twirled the tree around in my fingers. The carving reminded me of the tree back home housing my treehouse. A sturdy tree. Thick trunk. Embracing branches.

A flash of white raced across the field.

"Was that...?" I gasped as the predator in me longed to chase the animal.

"A unicorn. Aye."

"Rian." I dropped the carving on the ground as my jaguar shape fought to get free. My mouth watered. Hunger barreled to the forefront of my mind. "Pin me."

"Pin you?"

"Yes," I shrieked as fur burst from my arms. "Quickly."

My body contorted in an instant. Fur and claws burst free from my skin. I landed on my paws on the soft soil of the Summer Court. I raced across the fields chasing the unicorn. Its hooves glittered gold dust in its wake but that didn't matter to the hunger racing through my body. Each stride brought me closer to my prey. So close I lunged in the air intent on landing on the unicorn's haunches.

Midair, a body slammed into mine, pinning me to the ground. I growled and roared, thrashing under Rian's body. The golden stalks from the nearby field grew into a tall wall around us reaching up into the sky so high no jaguar could jump out. Rian uttered soothing words while laying on top of me. His comforting weight helped the predator instinct recede but not before I'd scratched him in my frenzy.

In time, I regained enough control to shift back.

"I'm so sorry, Rian," I said, brushing my fingers over the blood on his cheek and wiping away the evidence of my harm since the scratches had healed already. "I didn't mean to hurt you."

"Hush, my love, 'tis not your fault. I should have taken better care to feed you." He brushed back my hair. "You need meat, right?"

"Yes." I placed my hands over my bare stomach as a deep rumble exploded.

"You should tell me your needs as soon as you have them."

"I didn't want to ruin our happiness."

He eased me up into a sitting position. "You're not truly happy if you're hungry."

I dropped my head and stared at the ground.

Rian sighed. "Time for me to take you back to Earth."

"No." I gasped.

"We don't have to stay long." He unbuttoned his jacket and draped the soft fabric around my shoulders. "Long enough for you to eat if that's all you want."

I slid my arms into the long sleeves and guided the buttons in place. "What about your family?"

"I don't understand." He frowned.

"Should we tell them we're leaving?"

"Ah." He stood and held out his hand to me. "We could leave right here right now, but you are right. After everything Father has put in place to move forward, I should use his doorway."

I placed my palm in his and let him help me to my feet even though I was strong enough to leap a tall tree. This was nice having my mate take care of me. His jacket fell to my mid thighs which was more the length of the clothes I was used to wearing.

His palms glowed a bronze-gold of colors as he lowered the golden stalks to their original height. He squinted to the right.

"From what Father said about the doorway, the location should be a long walk that way."

"Makes sense." I set off walking. "Far enough away from your most vulnerable places."

Rian fell into step with me. "You look good in my jacket."

"I look good in anything according to you."

He chuckled. "I'm not wrong."

"You're biased."

"I have every reason to be."

"Come on, charmer, let's get this over with."

CHAPTER TWENTY

SOPHIA

After a longer-than-expected walk, we spotted the tower in the distance. A great white column rose into the baby blue sky. At the top of the tower sat a red roof almost like a beacon for people to find. I wondered at the design choice of colors, whether it was deliberate.

They'd stationed many guards dressed in their red attire on the outskirts of the field around the tower. In front of the building were two sets of guards. Swords with ornate hilts hung from scabbards strapped to their sides. Their red outfits matched the color of the tower's roof.

"Your Highness." A guard stepped forward. "How may we assist you?"

"Captain Finn," I greeted. "We're using the door to head to Earth for a short time."

His expression pinched. "I've received no word from the King."

"'Tis an urgent matter otherwise I would have informed the King myself. Please send a messenger to alert him of my leaving."

"Forgive me Prince Rian, but this isn't how they trained us to guard the doorway." He dipped his head.

My power surged to my hands making my crown swirl around my head. The guard took a step backward.

"I'll have two guards escort you." He snapped his fingers at the guards beside him.

"I can protect my mate," Rian growled.

"Rian," I said soothingly, placing a palm on his arm. "Guards are fine. We're going there without delay then coming back."

He dropped his gaze to me instead of glaring at the guards. His eyes skittered over my face before he nodded in agreement.

"Follow me," Captain Finn said.

He opened the heavy wooden door to the tower. Inside the air rushed like a blowing gale through the place. The hairs on the back of my neck stood on end. This wasn't like when Rian unlocked the Veil. The power inside this tower seemed wild.

Rian sucked in a harsh breath.

"It's been hard to contain the doorway of the Veil to these walls." Captain Finn grimaced.

Rian lifted his glowing hand to the swirling air. At once the gale-force wind dropped to a soft rustle and the pressure inside the tower eased.

"Father has been here every day?"

"Aye," he said.

"Good. The doorway needs his power. Mine will suffice for now." He stepped into the now bronze-gold-colored Veil, held out his hand to me, and waited for me to take it before asking. "Your jungle?"

I didn't even need to say yes before the Veil to the Summer Court closed around us and we were moving through the mist and walking out into the lush green Amazon jungle. A Howler monkey hollered at our intrusion from high in a banana tree. The guards drew their sharp-looking swords and readied themselves for an attack.

"It's a monkey," I said. "It won't hurt you. You can lower your swords."

The guards glanced at Rian, who nodded. They placed their swords back in the scabbards but kept their stances on alert. I was on alert too, for who knew what had happened to my colony after they thought I'd died? Maybe they'd fled or maybe someone killed them in my absence. Another queen might have taken over even though I possessed no heir. Whatever happened, I'd find out now I was here.

But the most pressing concern raging through my body was my hunger for meat. The Howler monkeys kept shouting their distress at our intrusion, which made me want to shut them up forever. I lifted my hands to the buttons on the shirt.

"Turn your backs," Rian demanded of the guards who'd come through the Veil with us.

They hesitated as any good guard would when tasked with protecting their liege.

"Now, unless you want me to gouge your eyes so you can't see until your eyes grow back."

The guards glanced at each other before they faced the jungle instead of us. I unbuttoned the jacket and handed it to Rian. The sweltering air coated my naked body in a damp mist in seconds.

"Promise I'll be as quick as I can." I tossed back the long length of my hair, already eager to shift into my jaguar form. "Find cover. Those two stick out like sore thumbs here in those red clothes."

Rian eyed the guards. "Aye. I should send them back."

"They wouldn't go," I said. "Besides, at least I know you're protected."

He scoffed. "I don't need protection. It's you I'm worried about."

"I'll be fine." My fingernails shifted into claws. "I'm made for hunting prey. What happened with the poachers was my fault. I should have known better than to attack when we didn't have eyes on all of them."

Rian scowled, but there was nothing else I could say that would convince him otherwise.

I let the shift complete. Fur burst through my skin in a sensual slide as my bones reshaped into a jaguar. I landed on my paws, nose lifting in the air, scenting the nearest target—the Howler monkeys. I slinked into the undergrowth of the fernery. The fronds tickled my sides, but I kept my focus on the monkeys up ahead. One slow creeping step at a time, I stalked my prey. The monkeys, no longer seeing my presence, quietened. Rian and the guards must have hidden too for them to stop sounding the alarm through the forest.

This was good.

An easy meal.

Then we'd travel back to the Summer Court.

We'd stop by the colony, and I'd see if everyone was all right. I needed to know that too. I didn't stop caring about them even though they believed I was dead.

The humid scent of the jungle filled my lungs trying to drown out the hint of monkey, but I'd locked my prey into my stalk. I paused. Up ahead I spotted the small shapes of the brown monkeys through the leafy fronds. Some sat on the ground picking bugs from each other's backs and eating them. Others scampered up the nearby banana trees. I surveyed the group looking for the weakest prey. A predator always searched for the easiest kill. The least exertion of energy for our food was preferable. I preferred taking out the weakest animal. One in its prime seemed like a waste, but an animal heading toward death already was right.

There. Sitting a small distance from the group sat an old monkey with gray hairs on his face. He hunched his shoulders as he rested his chin on his chest. His eyes were closed in daytime slumber. I inched around the group of active monkeys closer to my target. Paw by paw in freeze frame motion, I came within striking distance. I lunged through the fernery. Monkey screams rent the air. My jaws clamped around the old monkey a second after the animal lifted its head to the warning cry of its group. Fear flashed in the monkey's eyes for a second before the acceptance of its death.

Blood burst into my mouth in a warm gush, making me gulp the heated liquid. The other monkeys scurried away from the scene of death. I dragged the carcass into a nearby tree and, settling on a branch, I ate my kill. The incessant hunger of craving meat died with each bite. I ripped and tore at the flesh, chomping pieces through my sharp teeth. Soon there was nothing left of my meal.

I stretched out on the limb, content to bask in this satisfied mood for a short time.

The sound of a branch snapping jolted me to alert in an instant. A big black jaguar stalked under the base of the tree. I kept still, so I didn't give away my location. The jaguar sniffed the ground, scanned around, and then up. His amber eyes glowed through the greenery. I'd know those eyes anywhere. Laz.

I jumped down and landed in front of him. He reeled back, his paws flicking up leaf litter in his hurry to get away.

"Laz," I said into his mind.

He ceased his escape and faced me.

"Sophia?"

He padded closer. His nose sniffed mine as though my words in his head hadn't been enough to confirm who I was. My scent would do that.

"I thought you were dead."

He hung his head.

"I almost was according to Rian. Did you get the last poacher? The one who shot me."

"Yes. It's been months, Sophia. I thought you were gone for good."

"I'm fine now. How is everyone?"

Laz shifted. His black jaguar changed into a tall naked man. He didn't cover himself as he waited for me to shift too. I reclaimed my body, placing a hand over my breasts as I grabbed a fallen leaf from the nearest banana tree and wrapped it around my body like a dress. If Rian wanted to gouge out eyes, then I wouldn't put Laz in the firing line. A predator needed their eyes. Sure, he'd heal after a time but that would leave him at a disadvantage until he did so.

"None of us knew what to do," he said, scowling since I'd never cared about nudity before, but not asking me about the leaf.

"Understandable. I should have put a system in place for if I die. I suppose when being immortal and hard to kill I didn't think about it. Who's in charge now?"

"No one. It's a mess. Everyone is fighting each other. Some have left the colony now they don't have your protection. A rogue male is circling us trying to take females."

"Shit."

I longed to roar my frustration to the forest. How could I go straight back to the Summer Court now? What did this mean for me and Rian? Would we be back to being mates living in separate realms? I didn't want that, and I was certain he didn't either. Not now we'd enjoyed a taste of what life would be like living together as royalty.

"Let's head back to the colony. Once everyone sees you're alive, then they'll calm down," Laz said.

I paced away from Laz. I picked up a fallen branch and hurled the limb into the jungle. Leaves crunched under the fall of the solid timber. Birds startled into the air. Their wings were a vibrant display of reds, greens, and blues.

What about Rian? How could I do this to my mate?

"Laz. I don't know if I can."

"What the hell do you mean? You're our queen. It's your birthright to rule us."

I ran a hand through my hair, forgetting flowers now adorned my head as a crown. My fingers caught on one and my heart plummeted even more.

"What's with the flowers in your hair? Are you a hippy now?"

I almost laughed, but the gravity of the situation dragged me down. "It's my Fae princess crown."

Laz's eyebrows rose so high they disappeared under the thick fall of his dark hair. "How can you be both? The Queen of the Jungle and a Fae princess?"

I shrugged. "Beats me, but I am. How do I make this work?"

"Beats me," Laz said copying my words.

"You're no help." I folded my arms over the banana leaf, hating the way the foliage scratched my body. Nothing compared to the silkiness of Fae material. As much as I didn't like the length of the dresses, I loved the way they'd caressed my skin.

"I'm your second in command, not a miracle worker." He scowled. "All I know is your jaguar colony needs their queen. Do the Fae need you as their princess? Or is it your mate's needs you're putting first?"

"Why shouldn't I put my mate's needs first?" I huffed. "Or mine?"

"Run back to wherever you came from then." Laz threw his hands out. "Forget about us and how we'll die without you."

I sucked in a harsh breath. "Low blow, Laz. I care about every jaguar shifter. Even those rogue males. I don't want anyone to die."

"Prove it," he taunted.

CHAPTER TWENTY-ONE

RIAN

"*R IAN,*" Sophia's soft voice flittered through my mind.

"*Aye, my love?*"

"*There's a problem.*"

My powers surged in an instant to protect Sophia. Around me, the branches creaked as a wind of my making blew through the palm trees and the Monkey Brush with a whistling rustle. The guards, hiding in the fronds of a bush beside me exchanged a wary glance.

"*Are you hurt?*"

My most immediate concern. If someone injured Sophia here again, then I might do the same thing as my father and lock my mate away in the Summer Court. Sophia wouldn't be happy about it either.

"*No. It's the colony. I need to head there now.*"

"*Wait for me to join you.*"

"*I'm afraid it'll be better if I turn up by myself as their queen, not your Fae princess.*"

I sensed her reluctance to say those words through the sound of her voice inside my head. Was she thinking of staying here? Permanently? Were we doomed to always be apart?

"You have until I catch up with you."

"I'm faster than you through the jungle," came her amused reply. *"I'll see you at the colony."*

"You can be sure of that."

I severed the connection before I told her not to go without me. My feisty mate didn't need me dictating her life. I never had. I never would. She'd resent me if I did. Whatever was wrong with her colony, I needed to trust she'd fix it as their queen. Perhaps I'd been selfish to keep her in the Summer Court those few extra days when her people needed her.

"We're heading to the jaguar colony," I said to the guards.

They exchanged a nervous glance. It'd been way too long since Father's royal guards visited Earth. Not since their mass destruction of the Trappers. I often wondered about the night and what happened here on Earth. Father forbade me to join him in his quest to end the threat since I was next in line to the throne. Lorcan had been by his side, but he'd kept the details to himself, as had all the guards.

We walked through the jungle using our power to bend branches out of our way. I used the call of my mate's mating mark to guide me in the right direction since every species of tree and fern appeared similar. There was no pattern in the jungle. The plants dispersed themselves over an extensive area. One perk of placing a Fae mating mark was the fact we could trace our mate anywhere by it. Another reason choosing a mate wasn't something we did often. The connection between two marked mates was stronger than anything in existence.

Probably stronger than my powers.

Each step closer to Sophia called to my primal being. She might be the baser creature with her jaguar part, but I possessed a wildness too. The guards kept their duty to protect me seriously. They were on high alert as we walked into the colony. Jaguars, Sophia's soldiers, rushed forward ready to keep us at bay. The guards drew their swords.

"Stop," Sophia yelled from the balcony of her treehouse. "My mate and his guards are welcome here."

Laz strode in front of the soldiers and waved them down.

"Why do you have guards with you this time?" he asked.

"They're for Sophia's protection."

He scowled. "Why weren't they with her then?"

"A jaguar can't hunt with guards." I rolled my eyes at his lack of brainpower.

"Screw you," he muttered under his breath, so Sophia didn't hear him.

"Excuse me?" I leaned my ear closer. "I didn't quite catch what you said."

He shoved me in the chest. My guards drew their swords. Sophia landed on the ground beside us.

"What is wrong with you two?" she asked, stepping between us.

Laz firmed his lips. I didn't take my eyes off him. I still didn't trust him.

"Where were you when a poacher shot Sophia?" I asked as a sudden burst of anger fueled my power into a raging wind again.

"Right beside her, dick. Where were you?"

We lunged at each other, but Sophia held us back with a hand on each of our chests. Laz snarled. I curled my lip. He didn't scare me in his jaguar shape. I'd take him in either form. My powers were greater than his as a shifter.

Sophia stopped fighting against us and caught our shirts in her fists. She drew us toward her and growled. Instant arousal surged through me. I blinked away the blinding need of lust, but my vision turned hazy around the edges like Sophia was in a halo of light. The scent coming from her body was heady in a way I'd never smelled before. Her fingers loosened on our shirts.

"Oh, crap," she whispered, placing her hands over her breasts. "I so don't need this right now."

"What's wrong?" I asked.

"You're so useless," Laz snarled. "She's a jaguar going into heat, dumbass."

"Heat? Like the Fae have heats?"

I hadn't bothered to discuss the option for us to have a child since we both lived in two different worlds, so I hadn't learned the intricacies of the jaguar breeding cycle. Short-sighted on my part, but it'd seemed selfish to even consider a child when we lived in two different realms.

"Worse," Sophia said. "Jaguars have sex at least one hundred times a night until they produce a pregnancy."

I grinned. "Well, mate of mine. Let me get you pregnant."

Sophia laughed. "There are more pressing matters." She patted my chest. "This is perfect. I can use my heat scent to lure in the rogue jaguar, put him in his place, and integrate him into the colony."

"Are you crazy?" I asked as immediate concern for my mate barreled to the surface of my emotions. "You want to put yourself in the line of being attacked again? Did you learn nothing from hunting the poachers?"

Her eyes narrowed a fraction at a time until they were slits of green glaring at me.

Bit by bit I held up my glowing hands as my power fought to protect my mate. "I'm sorry. That was uncalled for. You know how to handle your people the best. I'll be by your side every step of the way."

Her face softened as she stepped forward and toyed with the buttons on my shirt. "I need you to stay here. Any male scent will deter the rogue jaguar and ruin my plan. I'll take Ana and Camila with me. They're both Lieutenants with plenty of experience. They'll have my back."

"But?"

"I'll draw the rogue back here to my soldiers if need be, but I'd rather avoid the men fighting. It's better if I put him in his place rather than have the males fight and go into a mating frenzy over who gets to mate with me."

I growled almost like a jaguar. "I'll fight anyone who thinks they can mate with you."

She sidled up to my body. "All this talk of fighting is getting me hot."

I cupped her elbows and drew her closer. My body surged with lust from the scent of the pheromones coming off her. I was ready to give her what she needed.

Laz exaggeratedly cleared his throat.

"Right." Sophia moved out of my embrace. "I'll be back soon. This won't take long. Trust me." She kissed my cheek and was off running into the jungle while shedding her clothes at the same time. Sophia disappeared into the green undergrowth before she was naked. At least I didn't have to gouge out anyone's eyes even if I possessed a pent-up rage right now. Her two Lieutenants ran after her shifting on the run as well.

My jungle queen was once again putting herself on the line to fight for her people. While I was proud of my mate, I hated every second she was missing from my sight. At least she had protection, but if something bad happened to her again, then I wasn't sure how I'd react. My hands sparked with enough power to set the jungle on fire or overflow the river to the tops of the trees or turn the sky black so no sunlight could get through my darkness.

Black like Sophia's fur.

Black like her hair.

She'd return victorious. This was her home. Her life. And I was a mere bystander.

CHAPTER TWENTY-TWO
SOPHIA

I T WASN'T THE FIRST occasion I'd been in heat, and this wouldn't be the last. This wasn't the first time I'd been in heat while mated to Rian either, but this was the first time he was aware of the cycle. I'd never informed him the other times because I hadn't wanted our child to choose which parent they'd go with when we always went our separate ways. Sure, we always came back together, but we'd never lived together.

Now I wanted to live with him more than anything in my life.

As for a child... well, I wasn't sure now was the right time. Would there ever be a right time? With Earth so unsettled. Jaguar shifters hiding who we were. Did I want to bring a child into that life? Rian's life in the Summer Court while idyllic exhibited problems too. But if mates used excuses to not have children, when did they ever have them? Because no time would ever be perfect.

And if the Fae were having problems reproducing, would that transfer to me since my mate was a Fae?

I rubbed up against a palm tree, scent-marking the area with the heady aroma of a jaguar in heat. A healthy male would be larger than me, but I was agile with a mountain of experience to defend myself against unwanted advances. I hunkered down ready for a fight.

Soft male chuffing came from my left. I growled in warning. The male jaguar kept coming even though my growl was clear I didn't want him. My pheromones would mess with his control and make it easier for me to beat him. He strutted into the open, tail high in the air along with his head. I bared my teeth. He curled his top lip scenting the air. I swiped a spray of dirt and leaves toward him. He charged. I lunged forward. He stopped before me growling. I growled back. For a split second, he hesitated. I took my opening and swiped my claws along his front leg. He fell to the ground, a howl of pain ripping from his throat.

"Stay down," I said. *"I'm your queen and you will obey me."*

He hissed. *"I don't need a queen."*

Glaring down at his fallen body, I moved into the kill position.

"I don't want to kill you, but I will. You've been terrorizing my colony and trying to steal my people." I bared my teeth. *"Submit to me. We have enough problems without fighting between our people."*

"I'm tired." He laid his head on the ground. *"All we do is hide or fight. We shouldn't live like this."*

"I agree. That's why I'm working to bring about a better life for all of us."

"How?"

"My mate is a Fae prince with untold power."

"A Fae? I don't believe you."

"He's marked me as his mate. Gave me a Fae crown. I'll shift and show you."

"You think he can help us?"

"I know he can."

The cat licked the wound on his leg while eyeing me. I gave him a moment to let my words sink in.

He changed shape and shifted into a man sitting on the ground.

I shifted too, once again using the nearest large leaf to cover my body. He rose his eyebrows.

"My mate will gouge out your eyes." I shrugged. "He's rather territorial."

"Understandable." He lifted his chin. "Is he really a Fae? They're like fairytales now."

"Yes, he is."

"I remember the stories we were told about the Fae. If one is back here on Earth, then there is a chance for us."

"More than a chance, but we need to unite, not fight between us."

He stood. "Agreed. I'll scour the jungle for the rest of the rogues and bring them to you."

I tilted my head. "Why?"

"I can't live in your colony. Your people will hate me for trying to steal them."

"My people will do as I tell them."

"If the Fae are back, then Earth is about to change. We need to change too. I'm Julius and I'll be your servant, Your Majesty."

I dipped my chin. He was right. With the King creating a doorway through the Veil so Fae could travel to Earth, then both realms were about to change. Earth hadn't experienced the help of the Fae for centuries and it showed. If the Fae came back and used their powers over nature, then Earth would heal. Reset itself to its once beautiful grandeur. A place where humans and supernatural creatures coexisted together in peace.

That was all any of us wanted.

We longed for the tales of old. Happiness and freedom. A place we'd all be safe from harm and destruction. I dug my toes into the damp soil sensing the vibrations of Earth. We were all connected to this place. We all needed to fix both realms. One piece at a time we'd heal. Joined as mates, fate was right, but when wasn't it?

Julius shifted into a jaguar and raced into the jungle. I let him go. He either believed as I did change was upon us, or I'd hunt him down or send my soldiers to end him. Rian was wrong thinking I put myself in the line of fire. I didn't. I always put myself in a position to make things better. Today I had.

Tonight, I'd prove that to him by returning unharmed.

I shifted and ran through the jungle eager to return to my mate and our future together. A shiver of excitement ran through my body. Damn hormones. I wanted to kiss Rain and make love to him, but if we started, we wouldn't stop for the rest of the night.

And then I'd end up pregnant.

I didn't want that. Did I?

I stalked through the jungle. The threat of the rogue male was over, but there were more out here in the expanse of the Amazon. One thing the place had in its favor was the sheer volume of land uninhabited by humans. Perfect for allusive jaguar shifters. It always surprised me other supernatural creatures hadn't set up territory here, and they'd chosen other places on Earth to hide their true identities. If we no longer needed to hide, we'd be free. If humans accepted the Fae for who they were, the protectors of Earth, instead of forgetting they even existed.

Each step back to the colony sent an awareness of Rian through my veins. The pounding beat of my heart set a fast rhythm to the pace of my paws. Dirt filled the gaps in my pads, but I paid little heed to the grainy soil. Rian was all I wanted. I sauntered into the colony. Laz and my soldiers stood on patrol, monitoring the surrounding jungle. They spotted me before Rian, but not by much. He spun fast. His eyes landed on me and ran the length of my body searching for wounds. When he found none, his gaze filled with adoration, which made me want him even more.

I shifted as I walked into his arms. He draped his jacket around my shoulders and embraced me.

"You're unharmed?"

"Of course." I squeezed his waist, then pushed back a fraction so I could do up the buttons on the jacket. "All sorted."

"I didn't doubt you, but I worried." He nuzzled my ear with his mouth. "Mmm, you smell good."

"It's the pheromones." I tugged his hair until he lifted his head.

His indigo-rimmed blue eyes sparkled with the same lust I was experiencing. I turned to Laz before I dragged Rian up to my treehouse and didn't come out until he impregnated me.

"Laz. The rogue tormenting the colony is gone. Spread the word through the settlement. Everyone can rest assured he submitted to me as his queen."

"Where is he then?" Laz squinted at the jungle.

"I sent him on an errand. He'll return in time."

Laz spoke to a soldier, who then climbed up the nearest trunk and ran from treehouse to treehouse informing every jaguar shifter in residence the rogue was no more.

"Now what?" Laz asked.

"We celebrate. Organize a communal feast for tonight."

I slid my arm through Rian's and urged him to fall into step with me. He did so willingly as though strings tied us together, but it was our hearts that connected us, and our mating marks. I longed to run my tongue over the permanent mark I'd placed on his neck when I'd claimed him. Somehow a little jaguar shifter magic found its way to Rian, just as his powers found their way to me. I touched a finger to one flower around my head nestled in my hair.

It would take everyone at least an hour to get ready.

For an hour I'd need to remind myself to *not* have sex with Rian.

Easy.

"What's easy, my love?"

Shit, did I think that last part aloud in my mind?

"Um, being back here."

I climbed hand over hand up the ladder to my treehouse. Rian followed behind me as did his guards, which was a tad disconcerting having them stay so close. Did his father think him incapable of protecting himself? Rian had been visiting Earth for many years behind the King's back with no harm coming to him. He could protect himself.

And me if it came to it.

I opened the door of my treehouse and walked into the place that had been my home for a long time. It didn't feel this way now. The Summer Court and the palace felt like home. I glanced around at my meager belongings in the single-room treehouse. A plump mattress lay on a platform in one corner. A shelf with a lantern beside the bed and scrolls of maps. On the other side by the window was a hammock made with bright red cotton strings. Comfortable for either of my shapes to lie in and watch the jungle below. A table made from twisted trunks of trees lined a wall and four chairs along the sides. The place I'd sat pouring over the maps of the jungle learning every place a poacher might hide while hunting us. A half dozen rocks sat on the table for me to weigh the corners of the maps down. Laz and Ana often sat at the table with me discussing the territory.

Rian had visited me here before, but they'd always been fleeting visits. A few days at most before he went back home to the Summer Court or in search of the origin of their Spring of Life. Now I'd seen the magnificence of their spring. Now I understood his determination to save it because I'd want to save the spring too even if it didn't hold the key to the Fae's immortality.

"I should change," I said, pointing at the set of drawers near the bed.

Rian eyed me as he shut the door behind him, closing the guards outside and leaving them on the balcony to protect us if need be.

I stripped off the jacket and tossed the garment at Rian. He caught it. His gaze heated as he looked his fill of my naked body.

"Are we going to talk about your heat?"

"No." I opened the drawer and slid on a pair of panties. "There's nothing to talk about. I've tolerated a heat before. It'll go away. I don't turn into a mindless sex maniac."

Rian cursed under his breath.

I fastened a bra and slid on a t-shirt. The rough cotton was alien on my body after the softness of the Fae fabric.

"My love, that's not what I meant." He pulled out a chair and sat at the table.

I tugged on a pair of shorts and yanked the zip into place almost catching my finger in my haste because I wanted to be a mindless sex maniac right now with Rian. To let my mating urges take over and have sex a hundred different ways until he impregnated me.

But a baby?

"I—"

"We," he whispered. "We're a 'we.'"

"We're torn. My people here need me. Your people there need you. We're always being yanked in opposite directions."

He sighed and placed his elbows on the table then rested his chin in his hands. "We are. I don't like it either."

"So what are *we* going to do?" I pointed back and forth between us.

"We do what's right like we always do. Royals put their people first. They drummed this into me from the time I could talk." He rubbed his chin in his hands. "Your people need you, so we'll stay here."

"But..."

"I can't separate from you ever again." He shook his head as though the thought of leaving me pained him. "I'd hoped to make our life together in the Summer Court, but your colony fell apart without their queen and I can't have that on my conscience. They're my people too now."

Tears threatened to fill my eyes as I swallowed the lump in my throat. "I wanted to remain in the Summer Court too."

"You did?" He lifted his head from his hands.

"It felt like home," I whispered.

He gave me a sad smile. "Perhaps one day the Summer Court will be our home. For now, we stay here. Together."

"What about your family?"

"I'll head back to the Summer Court and tell them. With the doorway open, it'll be easier for us to move between the realms. You won't have to spend every day here. A queen can travel and leave her second in command to oversee the colony. You're telepathic. Any time you're needed here in a hurry, we can return as swiftly as necessary."

"Laz won't like it."

"He should do as you say whether he likes it or not."

I bit my lip to stop myself from defending Laz, because Rian was right, as my General he should do as I say. If I left Laz to oversee the colony for a day or two, then everyone should listen to him as they had before when I'd ventured away from the colony on missions.

Rian scowled. His obvious dislike for Laz would be hard to live with.

"If we're staying here, then you need to get along with Laz because I can't have you two bickering all the time."

"I'll be civil, but one wrong move, and I'll end him."

Laz wouldn't hurt me. He was my second cousin. I rolled my eyes.

"All right, my overprotective mate. I need to head down for the feast. Are you coming or heading to the Summer Court?"

He stood. His nostrils flared as he drew in a deep inhale.

"Since you won't discuss having a child with me, I'll head to the Summer Court now." He inhaled again. "You may act civilized, but your scent is turning me into a raging sex beast. If I stay around you, then I'll have to taste the aroma coming from between your legs, and once I do..."

I sucked in a desire-filled breath. Oh, how I wanted him to do all those things. Lock the door and not come out until we were both exhausted.

Instead, I nodded. "I'll see you in a day."

CHAPTER TWENTY-THREE
RIAN

O NE GUARD STAYED WITH Sophia, and one guard returned to the Summer Court with me even though I'd wanted them both to stay with her. It was easier returning home with the doorway in existence. Almost as easy as it'd once been before Father placed the lock on the Veil. As we stepped through the Veil into the tower, another set of guards came into view. They'd raised their swords ready to defend the Fae kingdom.

I almost laughed. Only a Fae or a marked mate of a Fae could pass through the Veil. If they were a threat, then we were all doomed. Besides, was there even any Fae left on Earth? Father sent out a call to the Fae he was sealing the Veil, so I'd assumed with the influx of Fae they'd all left Earth. Perhaps I'd assumed wrong?

We'd been wrong about a lot of things.

It was wrong to leave my mate while she was in heat. I should be having sex with her right now. Pleasuring her and taking away the need I sensed humming through her body. She may have acted strong like her heat didn't matter, but I knew otherwise.

The guard led me out of the tower, and I made my way back to the palace through the fields enjoying the warmth of the Summer Court sun, the caress of the breeze, and the absolute perfection of the realm. Sophia surprised me by admitting she wanted to stay here. I'd thought I'd have to fight for her to choose my home, but when the choice came, it was me agreeing to live with her. I couldn't live without her ever again. Not after I'd almost lost her. A shudder of dread ran through me.

She was safe with her colony. With her soldiers. Plus, she had a Fae guard who controlled the power of ice. He'd be able to freeze anyone or anything heading her way.

Each footstep on my home soil soothed my powers as I connected them to this realm, but my powers also enjoyed being on Earth. There was a unique sensation in them there. As though they were begging me to use them. I'd only used them to help myself or my mate while on Earth. I'd never used them for the greater good as the Fae had in the olden days.

The palace rose ahead like a homing beacon. Great turrets and walls sparkled in the sunlight. The windows almost appeared to wink at me. As I walked up the entrance, the front doors opened before I made it to them, Roisin rushed out and hugged me.

"You're back safe," she said.

"Aye, you have nothing to worry about." I patted her head.

She ducked out of my reach and scowled. "Stop treating me like a little kid."

"You are little. You're only fifty years old."

She placed her hands on her hips. "And to think I'd made you and your mate a painting."

I grinned. "Sophia will love that."

"Where is she?" Roisin peeked over my shoulder.

"On Earth. We've chosen to stay there for now. Her people need her."

"We need you here." She huffed.

"I'll be back often. The doorway will be handy. You could come to visit too."

She bit her lip. "I've never been to Earth."

"I know."

"Do you think Father will let me go?"

I grimaced. "Doubtful, but perhaps in time. Let's see how this doorway goes first, then we'll work on the rest."

She nodded. "One day we'll be whole again."

Rosin turned and walked toward the rose garden. She loved the place and was often painting the roses. She'd most likely set an easel up ready to go. I'd miss seeing her artistic flare every day. I'd miss all my family. How hard must it be on Saoirse separated from all of us when we'd been together for so long? I'd have to visit her too while I lived on Earth.

Those words didn't even compute.

Me living on Earth.

A Fae prince.

Father might revoke the doorway when I told him.

I hurried into the palace intent on getting the inevitable debate over with. No matter what Father said, I needed to be with my mate. He'd understand. Wouldn't he? I nodded at the servants as I passed by them. Dinner preparations were well underway, and it may be my last meal with the family for a while.

Grunts and groans, followed by the sound of wooden staffs hitting each other came from the courtyard. I ventured under the golden arches. Aislinn and Briana were sparring. Their staffs twirled fast and furious as they struck at each other. Blows hit here and there but for the most part, my sisters avoided the other's advances. Briana was more of an expert with the staff than Aislinn, so her blows landed true and hard when she wanted. Aislinn spat blood on the floor from a split lip. She reached for her daggers and tossed two in quick succession at Briana. Briana dove to the ground not a moment too soon. The daggers landed in the column closest to me.

Aislinn strolled over, extracted one dagger from the column, and sheathed the blade in the holster strapped around her waist.

"Perhaps try not to cheat next time," I said.

Aislinn retrieved another dagger and flicked it around her fingers. "I didn't cheat."

"A staff fight should be just that."

"Father taught us to use whatever we possessed to win." She pointed the dagger at my chest.

"True," I said, putting my hand on the top of the blade and pushing the sharp tip downward. "Use your powers next time. You don't bother with them when fighting, why?"

"Blades are vicious looking. No one can see air."

"But they sense it. Use your power."

"He's right," Briana said, joining us. "Looking vicious won't win you a fight."

"I know how to be vicious," she snarled, then stomped out of the courtyard.

Briana let out a huff. "Her anger will harm her one day."

"It already does." I squinted after Aislinn's retreating form, but she wasn't coming back. "How's Saoirse? Have you seen her of late?"

"I snuck to Earth yesterday. She's doing well and so is their baby." A dreamy look came over her face. "I told Sledge next time I'm in heat I want to make a baby."

"Do you intend to tell everyone you have a mate first?" I smirked.

"Soon," she said. "Father is sending Lorcan to Earth to convince Saoirse to come home. Once she does and everyone accepts her mate, then I can announce mine. I think if we pushed Father too fast, he'd crack again. He seems like he's back to himself now."

I grimaced. "So, me telling him I'll be living on Earth with my mate might push him back into being overprotective?"

"You're what! Dia." She rubbed her forehead, hard and fast, sending a flower from her crown to the floor. "I don't know, Rian. Can't you live here?"

"We both want to, but we can't yet. Her people need her."

"Commendable," she said. "I understand. Sledge's people need him as their Alpha, but he can pass on the title if he chooses. Can't she do the same?"

"No. She's royalty like us. Born to the position. Only another born to the title will rule the jaguar people."

"Your child then."

"Aye, but she doesn't want a child."

"I'm sure that's not true."

"She's in heat now, but she won't conceive with me."

Briana laughed.

"What's so funny?"

"When I was in heat, Sledge demanded I mark him so we wouldn't conceive a baby. He recognized I wasn't ready."

"Are you saying she said no because I'm not ready?"

She chuckled. "Your mate would know, not me."

I scowled. Was she right? Was I the one not ready for a child to be brought into our lives when I wasn't even sure how long my Fae life would be anymore? I didn't want to leave my child alone without guidance and love. I wanted what I had with my parents. A long, long time with them.

"Where's Father? I must speak with him and head back to Earth."

"Last I saw, he was heading to the men's chambers with Lorcan to discuss secret men's business." She waggled her fingers.

I laughed. "You women have your sitting room too where you keep your secrets."

"We do, big brother. I'm heading there now." She smiled slyly. "I wonder what secrets I'll be telling?"

As we parted ways, I let out a groan. She headed toward her secrets, and I headed toward mine. Except I didn't have any secrets to keep anymore. Everything was out in the open, but I'd Briana's secret mating to keep. All being well, not for much longer.

Walking up to the chamber door, I raised my hand and rapped my knuckles against the wood in the pattern alerting those inside to my presence. One knock followed by two quick raps, then a set of three long knocks.

The door swung open and Lorcan let me into the room, closing and locking the door behind me. Father sat on one of the large chairs looking pinched in the face, but when he spotted me, he smiled.

"Rian, I'm happy to see you've returned safe and well." He waved a hand at the other chairs.

Lorcan and I sat in them. An orange flame flickered from the fireplace. The only fireplace in the castle that had housed a fire since that night because no women were allowed in here. The flames were a sign Lorcan started the fire since he loved fire so much and wielded it with ease. We didn't need the heat since Fae didn't feel the cold, but the atmosphere was soothing even if fire brought back bad memories of a time we all wished had never happened.

"Briana said you're sending Lorcan to fetch Saoirse home."

"I am. He leaves tomorrow." He rubbed a hand down his thigh. "I figured it would be better for me to send her favorite brother in my stead."

"She'd be happy to see you."

"You cannot know that. I behaved appallingly toward her. She was within her rights to gut me as she did." He grinned. "I'm lucky she didn't take off my head."

"Saoirse gutted you?"

Lorcan placed his hands behind his head and grinned.

"Aye," Father said. "I trained her well."

"Well, ah, I suppose it is better for Lorcan to go." I shot my brother a look.

He kept grinning like this was the most amusing thing he'd heard.

"The doorway will prove its worth," Father said.

"It was easier to come home with it," I admitted. "I hope to use the doorway all the time now."

Father frowned. "Why?"

"My mate and I need to live on Earth." I held up a hand as he opened his mouth. "For now. We intend to make our home here one day."

The silence in the room was thick and oppressive. Father's powers surged to his hands in a silver glow. Rian's hands glowed too, as he responded to the King's powers. My powers lurched for the surface, but I shoved them back. Bickering amongst us wouldn't fix anything.

"She's their queen, Father. What would you have her do? Abandon them?"

He drew his powers back with a long sigh.

"She's my mate. I belong with her."

"I'm not happy about you living there." Father leaned forward and placed his hand on my knee. "The moment you believe it's not safe, come home."

"Believe me, any threat to her and I'll have her here so fast she won't even know we've crossed the Veil."

Father chuckled and squeezed my knee. "The things we do for our mates."

"And we wouldn't have it any other way," I said.

CHAPTER TWENTY-FOUR
SOPHIA

S MALL ORANGE FLAMES FLICKERED over the coals in the firepit. Everyone pitched in to make a feast. A deer roasted on the spit over the fire, as a couple of people turned the handle to cook the meat. We might like raw meat in our jaguar form, but we enjoyed cooked meat when in our human shape. We spent most of our time as people, so we ate like people.

On another fire pit, fish sizzled. Others had collected an assortment of fruits and nuts and laid them on the long trestle table in the center of our community. Deep purple passionfruit, acacia berries, and the bright yellow aguaje fruit that tasted like carrots sat in wooden bowls. Beside them were a collection of Brazil and cashew nuts. At least if Rian returned sooner than he expected, he'd find plenty of food to eat. The fruit was abundant in the Amazon jungle so he wouldn't go hungry as I had in the Summer Court.

I suppose us living here on Earth made more sense, but I still wanted to live in the Summer Court one day. My dietary requirements would make that difficult, but as Rian said, we could come back and forth without difficulty now the Fae King had created a door, and his family and the Fae people accepted me as his mate.

I moved from person to person, talking to them, reassuring them I was there to protect them from any threat that might come at us. That the rogue jaguar males would no longer bother us. Poachers would still come for us. They'd always come while the humans had forgotten about supernatural creatures. I soothed the most anxious, telling them how great the Fae's powers were and now they'd returned to Earth, the humans would return to the olden days and worship them. The Earth would grow plentiful. People wouldn't need to kill us for our pelts to put food on the table for their families.

I hoped I told the truth.

We were a long way from that happening, but this was my hope. If the humans had the Fae to look up to, then they'd stop fighting each other and us. If they had the Fae fixing all the problems on Earth, then there'd be no need to fight. Earth would be like the Summer Court. A utopia.

I sold my dream, for I believed in it.

Laz sat on the edge of the party, a deep scowl on his face. I excused myself and wandered toward him, but he sighted me coming and stomped into the jungle. *What was his problem?* I tracked him through the jungle until

I found him by a small pool of water tossing stones into it.

"What are you doing out here?" I asked.

He jerked with a start, slamming his fist into the water, and sending up a spray over himself.

"I don't buy what you're selling." He kept flicking the water sending droplets onto the dirt.

"I'm not selling anything." I folded my arms.

"This Fae crap is just that. Look at you. You don't even look like a jaguar shifter anymore with those flowers in your hair."

"Laz!" I exclaimed, shocked he'd say such a thing.

He stood and dusted off his knees. "A Fae is no mate for the Queen of the Jungle."

"Rian is my fated mate." I tapped my fingers on my arm. "You can't argue with fate."

He prowled from the edge of the pool toward me. The hairs on my arms stood on end. I resisted the urge to take a step back. For the first time in my life, I didn't trust Laz.

"I can," he snarled, sounding more jaguar than person now.

I resisted the urge to shift so I could put him in his place. Being in jaguar shape would throw off more pheromones and send a male jaguar crazy. I'd be able to beat him like I did the rogue jaguar, but this was Laz, my second cousin. I didn't want to fight him.

"Laz, you need to calm down."

He prowled closer. "I'm very calm."

"Then you need to think."

"You should have a jaguar mate. Someone who will give you a jaguar child. The next Queen of the Jungle."

"I'm mated. No one is giving me a child but my mate," I snarled, fed up with Laz acting like an idiot.

"Your mate's not here. Yet again, but I am."

I inched back as the threat became clear. Laz wanted me as his mate. How hadn't I seen it? No wonder Rian didn't like him. He'd sensed the threat long before me. How stupid was I? I should never have let Rian return to the Summer Court without me, and without a doubt not while I was in heat. If Laz did the unthinkable, then I'd conceive his child. I couldn't let that happen. Snapping my claws out of my fingertips, I inched closer to the nearest tree. I'd climb it if need be.

Where was the damn Fae guard when I needed him? I'd slipped by him with no trouble out into the jungle. Stealth came effortlessly to jaguars. I hadn't even thought I'd need the guard, and here I was wishing he was with me.

Wishing Rian was with me even more.

Wishing I was anywhere but here.

Stop hesitating and strike.

"Sophia? What are you talking about?"

Fuck, I'd said that in my mind.

My heart raced a million beats per minute. What did I tell Rian? If he learned about Laz, he'd kill him. My distraction cost me. Laz lunged, slamming his body into mine and forcing me back into the rubber tree. My head cracked on the trunk as he pinned my body hard. I raked a claw across his face, slicing open a gaping wound in his cheek but missing his eye. Rian's words about eye gouging came back to me and I almost laughed.

This was insane.

Laz was attacking me.

His family.

His queen.

I roared and dug my claws into the back of his skull. His head thrashed from side to side as he tried to dislodge me, but he didn't let up with the pressure of his body. He slapped at my hand in a futile attempt to dislodge my hold, but then dug his claws into the back of my hand realizing a hand wasn't enough to get me to release him. I let go with a cry of outrage. I shifted under him. My body fell to the jungle floor on a set of paws ready to run, but a blinding bronze-gold glare surge of power flared behind us.

Laz's body rose in the air through an invisible force. He kicked and thrashed, yelling the entire time as though he was in great pain.

I blinked through the blinding light. Rian stood in the center. His face was a murderous mask. One I'd never witnessed before.

"You dared to touch my mate," he growled. "Hurt her."

In an instant, Laz's body twisted in the air as the force from Rian's powers appeared to press in on him so fast and brutally that his stomach dipped, as did his chest. Laz screamed until he couldn't scream anymore. His body crumpled in on itself as Rian used his powers over the very air to crush him. His heart stopped so fast it happened in the blink of an eye.

I should have stopped Rian from killing Laz. I should have been the one to give him his punishment. As his queen and his victim, but right now I was in shock. I'd trusted Laz. He was family. Tears filled my eyes. Rian glanced at me. His expression turned even more murderous. Long after the screams died, Rian's powers glowed from his hands. He tossed Laz's body on the ground. I eyed the twisted, bloody mess of his body in a detached sort of way I wasn't sure was good.

My body trembled. Tears blinded my eyes.

Rian walked bit by bit toward me, his glowing palms out so I could sniff them. I didn't need to. I always smelled the unique scent of my mate. My mate who'd just killed for me. Taken out the threat when I couldn't.

He dropped to his knees, slid his palms into my fur, and stroked my back.

"Easy, my love," he murmured over and over.

I dropped my head into his lap and closed my eyes. He petted me until the trembling stopped and I shifted in his arms. Rian gathered me closer still into the warmth and comfort of his chest, wrapping his arms around my body.

"I'm sorry," I whispered.

"'Tis not your fault." He picked up my bloody hand and kissed the wounds. "We should get Saltine to see to these."

I shook my head. "She left."

"When?" He frowned.

"When I did. It doesn't matter, they'll heal in a day."

"A day is too long for you to be injured."

"I should have listened when you said you didn't trust him," I said as I clung to his body with my arms never wanting to let him go. An exhale left my lungs before I said, "I didn't think he'd..."

"Neither did I." He ground his jaw. "But it's not your fault. You don't need to apologize to me. Or anyone. A man should never attack a woman."

"You're right." I dug my fingers into the firm muscles of his back. "Take me home."

He stood with me in his arms and walked toward the colony.

"No, I meant the Summer Court. I can't be here. Not after this."

"My love," Rian whispered. "You're stronger than this."

"I'm not." I sniffed. "This is too much. I want to be selfish and hide from the horrors of this life here on Earth."

"One thing I know is we can't hide forever. Look what happened from the Fae hiding. I won't let you run and hide and make the same mistakes as us. Your people need you. I need you. But most importantly you need to do this for yourself. You'll never forgive yourself if you hide."

I snuggled against his warm chest, letting the tingle of his power cleanse my body. He picked up my hand and kissed the wound Laz inflicted in our tussle. Rian was right. I lifted my head and met his eyes.

"Take me to the ceremonial cave."

"But we're already mated."

"This time we'll use the cave to conceive a child."

"Are you sure?" He searched my eyes for any hint of doubt.

"I am. I want a future with you. What better future is there than one as a family?"

CHAPTER TWENTY-FIVE
RIAN

"N o," I said even though every ounce in my body wanted this with Sophia.

"No?"

"Aye, I'm sorry, my love." I lowered her to her feet. "Now is not the time for us to create a child with your enemy lying dead at our feet. I don't want to conceive a child and for that to be your memory of how we made him or her."

Sophia dropped her gaze to the ground. Her defeated manner irritated me. I slid my hand under her chin and tilted it back up.

"I want you, and I want to give you a child, but not like this. When we do this, I want it to mean something special between us."

She swiped her tongue over her lips. I pressed a chaste kiss on her mouth.

"Maybe you're right," she said. "I wanted to take the tarnish of the night away."

"You will, but not how you think. We'll head back to the colony, your head held high, and you'll tell your people of Laz's betrayal. How together as one we defeated him and how we'll defeat everyone who comes to destroy us."

A tiny smile tugged at the corners of her mouth. "Naked?"

I swept a glance down her naked body. This was who she was. A jaguar shifter. I couldn't have her worried about hiding her true self for fear of my jealous rage.

"Aye." I swept a finger over one flower in her crown.

She shuddered under my light caress.

"What about gouging out eyes?" She let out a tiny laugh.

"I'll refrain."

A surge of energy filled the jungle. A dozen Fae guards in their red coats surrounded us. Sophia's eyebrows rose.

"Looks like Father sent reinforcements." I nodded at the head guard.

He stepped forward, wisely avoiding looking at Sophia's naked body.

"His Highness, we're ready to defend you and Her Highness."

"Stand down. I ended the threat." I waved him off.

"The King has demanded we are under your command and Her Highness's."

"Very well." I rubbed Sophia's back. "We're heading back to the colony now. You may accompany us."

Sophia shook her head. "Now we have a Fae army?"

"We may well need them."

"They need new clothes. The red is ridiculous here."

"They do. They'll fit in and be an asset."

"If you say so." She gave them another skeptical glance. "What should we do with Laz's body? We bury our dead. What do Fae do?"

I called my power to my hands, reveling in the task of disposing of Laz's body. He was one threat I was glad to be over with. Bronze-gold hues swirled in the soil around his body. The dirt moved like quicksand sucking Laz into the soil and sinking beneath the tiny granules until not a speck of him remained. As an added measure I called forth more plant life, making the passion fruit vine nearby burst into bright purple flowers, a minute later the blooms bared the reddish plum globes of the fruit.

Sophia squatted, placing her hands on the ground.

My power kept surging over the nearest trees and plants until the area glowed a vibrant green like the recent shoots of plants after a spring rain. Delicate orchids in a pale lavender color burst through the surface releasing the sweet scent of vanilla into the air. Up above in the branches of a tree, Bromeliads burst into vibrant red bloom. The Acacia's palms burst into thick black berries hanging from under the fronds of the leaves.

She peered up at me. "You healed the Earth."

I shrugged like it was no big deal to use my power this way.

She stood in a rush. "You don't understand, Rian. You settled the vibrations here. It's soothed. Healed. This is big. You made a difference to Earth."

I resisted the urge to shrug again. What brief surge of power I'd imbued in this place was nothing compared to what my powers could truly do. The Fae King's powers were even more astounding, but I kept that piece of information to myself since my mate was looking at me like I was the answer to every problem.

"I can't wait to tell everyone." She almost skipped through the jungle.

I shook my head as I followed her. The guards spanned out through the jungle protecting us from every angle. I was relieved Father sent them. It wouldn't hurt to have more eyes and ears around here. More protection for my mate. No poacher would get within reach now. I'd make sure of that.

We came out of the jungle to a bunch of curious looks from her colony. Sophia stood proud in all her naked glory while I battled the urge to gouge out everyone's eyes. I'd never get used to her being naked in front of others, but I'd live with it while in the jungle. Back in the Summer Court would be a different matter, but she'd admitted to liking Fae material, so I doubted she'd have a problem with me insisting she wear clothes there.

Her people were concerned when she told them the story of Laz. Her Lieutenant Ana stepped forward.

"My Queen." She dipped her head. "I'd like to head your contingency now."

Sophia eyed the woman from head to toe.

"Ana. I'll take your application under consideration." She clasped the woman's hand. "Let's finish eating all this wonderful food. We have new Fae guards to welcome too."

Ana walked over to the Fae guards along with a few other jaguar shifters. Soon everyone was mixing. Even though the Fae King's guards were on alert, they were polite to the jaguar shifters. I couldn't have made a better integration of the Fae back on Earth. As we ate the copious amounts of food, I didn't stray from Sophia's side. She'd dressed again in a pale green t-shirt and khaki shorts. Sophia was always looking to blend in with the surrounding nature. I made note of the color clothes the Fae guards would need. I'd send one guard back home to get the seamstresses to work on suitable attire. There was a lot to accomplish, but we'd get there.

As the night darkened, shifters ventured up to their treehouses. Sophia offered the Fae guards Laz's house to rest in and they set up a roster of who was on duty and who was off duty to rest. With the double protection of both our people on patrol, I relaxed and followed Sophia up to her treehouse.

The instant the door closed, Sophia stripped her clothes and climbed into bed. I undressed, eyeing the way she'd curled into herself under the white sheet. My mate wasn't happy, even if she'd appeared over the moon to every one of her people. Her mask was perfect, but I saw through it.

"My love," I whispered, sliding under the sheet, and gathering her into my arms. "We'll be happy here."

She sat up and tugged the mosquito net into place around us. The sheet fell, leaving her perfect breasts on display for my hungry eyes. Her scent was still ripe with pheromones, making my cock harden against my stomach.

"I'll make sure we are," she said.

"My feisty little jaguar queen." I drew her onto my chest and traced circles on her back. "Tomorrow we'll set more things in place, and we need a brief visit to the Summer Court."

"What for?" She snuggled close, laying her head on my chest.

"I left rather abruptly, and Roisin painted us a picture. She'd be upset if I didn't bring her painting here with us."

"Your sister made us a painting? That's so sweet."

"It'll brighten up your place."

Sophia laughed. "I do lack decorating skills."

I laughed with her. Kissed the top of her head and fought the urge to ravish her body. She wouldn't be in heat forever. I could last a day.

CHAPTER TWENTY-SIX
SOPHIA

R IAN AND I BARELY slept. Constant arousal made it impossible to relax and not think about sex with my sexy mate. We whispered to each other instead. The darkness of the night made our time more intimate to share our thoughts and feelings. Love filled our words and our touches. Each breath we took synched. Every beat of our hearts echoed the others.

Being with my fated mate like this was so right.

As the sun rose so did we. We dressed and made our way down the rope ladder. A flurry of activity was already filling the colony. Hammers and saws clanged through the jungle as another treehouse was being made for the Fae guards. I was glad my people took it upon themselves to welcome our additional guards. They sensed the change in the Earth the same way I did with the Fae here. Earth welcomed them.

I placed Ana as my second in charge. She'd been a good soldier and Lieutenant General in my battle against the poachers, now she'd be the General.

I drew Rian away from the colony and into the jungle. Guards followed us, but I ignored them as I headed toward the ceremonial cave. Rian didn't question me as we came to the entrance and ducked inside. Rian motioned for the guards to stay at the entrance.

"Remember when we first came here?" I prowled around the glittering cave like a jaguar about to pounce on its prey.

I was, in a way.

"Vividly." He grinned. "The week is my fondest memory."

I laughed. The sound echoed in the cave, bouncing off the walls and filling the place with happiness.

"Mine too." I prowled up to him. "Let's see if we can beat it."

Rian laughed and hauled me into his arms. His mouth devoured mine. I met his tongue stroke for stroke as we kissed in a heated passion. I tore at his clothes, shredding the fabric with my claws and leaving them in ribbons on the floor of the cavern. Rian met my hunger with his own, ripping my t-shirt from my body and then yanking my shorts down my legs.

He lowered us to the ground.

"I need a taste," he said.

"I need you too."

He laid back. "Sit on my face. We can do both together."

I turned around and eyed the proud erection straining against his stomach. A drop of pearly liquid sat on the tip. My mouth watered to taste him. I spun around and did as he said, lowering myself on his face as I laid against his stomach and slid his cock into my mouth. His tongue licked me in a frenzied manner until stars danced in my eyes. I clutched his hips trying to stay anchored to him while I sucked his hardness inside my mouth. Every muscle in my body tightened to the point of pleasurable pain. So fast he worked me toward an orgasm that I couldn't hold it back even though I wanted him to come inside my mouth too. My hips jerked as I came all over his tongue and face. He lapped me through the peak of pleasure, tugging me closer to taste all of me. Every inch he licked like a beast. My wild Fae prince when he was like this. Usually so refined unless he was loving me.

"Again," Rian growled.

I held onto his thighs as his lips and tongue worked my oversensitive clit. I sobbed around his cock, still in my mouth, and through the pleasure as another orgasm built and burst free. Rian rolled me to the ground taking a long lick over my inflamed flesh. His cock sunk into my throat, and he came with a shudder spilling inside me. I lapped at his taste, pleased I'd given him pleasure too.

For hours we tasted each other. Licked every inch of my body as I licked his in between orgasms too. My body was on fire. So aware of him, his touch, and his tongue that every stroke made me jump. After a long time, Rian took his cock in his hand and gazed at my dripping entrance. Could I even come again?

"Are you still in heat?" he asked in a voice rough with need.

I shook my head. Somewhere between my first and twentieth orgasm, my heat ended.

"All I can taste is you." He licked his lips. "Are you sure?"

"I'm sure. But I don't think I can come again." I flopped my head back on the floor of the cave.

Rian stroked his cock, squeezing the head until pre-cum seeped from the end. "You will. I'll make sure of that."

My insides clenched with need. The sight of Rian touching himself always turned me into a puddle of need.

"That's what I'm afraid of." I sighed.

He chuckled and lowered his body over mine until the head of his cock nudged my sensitive flesh. Every inch of my body screamed at me to take him deep. Let him fill me until he was the only thing I experienced inside me. I opened my legs wider. He pressed forward, inching his cock into my slick heat. I shuddered through every tiny movement until he seated himself and ground his hips, rubbing against my inflamed clit once again.

"Oh, God," I moaned.

"Rian," he husked out. "Or mate."

I couldn't even laugh. He fucked me in earnest. His cock caressed the places deep inside where his tongue and lips hadn't been able to. My muscles quivered at the friction, sending my heart racing so fast I thought I might pass out. For what seemed like hours, our sweaty bodies moved as one. Another orgasm built, but the release always seemed just out of reach. I almost told him I was right that I couldn't come again.

He slid his hands over my breasts. A soft bronze-gold glow illuminated his palms. The power of his touch turned my nipples into hard buds. He squeezed the tips until I bucked my hips, desperate for the orgasm tugging between my nipples and clit with each pull on my breasts. And then the release was there. A blinding wave of pleasure took everything I ever was with it. There was only me right here, right now. Me and my mate.

Rian squeezed my nipples, making my core clench tighter on him. His body jerked as he came deep inside me. Filling me with his semen that would one day make a child. Not today though. Today this was about us. About accepting our life here on Earth.

Whatever the future had in store, then we'd always be together. Here or the Summer Court. It didn't matter so long as we stayed together.

Rian rolled off me and lay with me on his chest. He stroked my back as my heart fought to come back to normal. As my vision and hearing did too.

After recovering, I lifted my head and gazed into his eyes. "This clothes thing might be a problem."

Rian laughed making me bounce on his chest.

"I'm going to say, your wandering around naked might save you having to get new clothes all the time."

I rolled my eyes. "What about you?"

"You want me to wander around naked too?" He rose an eyebrow.

I slapped his chest. "No. Definitely not. But next time, how about we undress like civilized people?"

He laughed harder. "You and I are not civilized."

I laid my head back on his chest. "True. So, um, can the Fae seamstresses make us more clothes? I feel bad I ripped yours to shreds again."

"They already are, my love."

"You're so smug." I grinned.

"And you love it."

I bit my lip, then said, "I love your cockiness and cock."

Rian's cock twitched between our bodies. I scrambled off his body. Rian rose and prowled toward me, the glimmer in his eyes an invitation for more sex.

"We have things to do," I said.

"My list of things to do are you." He caught me by the waist. "The rest will still be there in a few hours. Let me love you longer."

I sank into his embrace. He was right. The colony wasn't going anywhere for the next few hours. We could return to the Summer Court at any time. Rian wouldn't be able to heal the Earth in one day. And we still hadn't found the source of the spring. So much to do, but we possessed time to tackle the problems together, and now we had an alliance.

Fae and the jaguar shifters.

And with two of his sisters mated to wolf shifters, then there were even more of us working together.

Soon we'd fix all our problems. I believed that as much as I believed in my fated mate. The love of my life.

"Okay," I said. "But this time it's my turn to see how many times I can make you come."

Rian opened his arms. "Challenge accepted."

I grinned. "Isn't the challenge mine?"

"Mine, yours, we're both winners here, my love."

And win we would. Together. Forever.

FATED MATES OF THE FAE ROYALS

1. Fae's Song

2. Fae's Wolf

3. Fae's Alpha

4. Fae's Heart

5. Fae's Witch

6. Fae's Dream

7. Fae's Fate

8. Fae's Love

ACKNOWLEDGMENTS

First, thank you to my family for putting up with me disappearing into the world of books. To Belinda, thank you for encouraging me to write again after I lost everything in a computer crash. Remember to back up! A lot of work goes into creating a story, and I'm always thankful for the support of my online writing buddies, beta readers, and fellow authors, Immy for always making me smile, Tammy for believing in me from the start, Karen for being willing to read any level of heat I write. Cassie for her hand holding. Lana for her invaluable knowledge. Also, my fabulous beta reader Erica and her help with US English. The biggest thank you goes to my 'twin' Dannielle, who is the best critique partner, cheerleader, and sounding board ever, and is forever fixing my comma errors, sorry Dannielle I'm afraid you're stuck with them and me. Finally thank you to all you romance readers. You are my tribe.

ALSO BY

FANTASY AND PARANORMAL ROMANCE
Summer Court

Fae's Song

Fae's Wolf

Fae's Alpha

Fae's Heart

Fae's Witch

Fae's Dream

Fae's Fate

Fae's Love

Anthologies

Reluctant Bride

Alpha Male

ABOUT AUTHOR

Helen Walton is a tea drinking, chocoholic, romance writer. Stories are her obsession. She adores creating sensual romances containing a sprinkling of humor and the all-important happy ending. She lives in South Australia with her family, and menagerie of quirky animals where they all take her away from her book world and demand to be fed. Lucky for them, she enjoys cooking but prefers baking.

Sign up for my newsletter for exclusive content.

https://www.helenwaltonauthor.com/newsletter

Visit my website

https://www.helenwaltonauthor.com/

Follow me

BB   bookbub.com/profile/helen-walton

f   facebook.com/Helen-Walton-Author-1034966677 06602/

g   goodreads.com/author/show/20249188.Helen_Walton

◎   instagram.com/helen.walton.author

♪   tiktok.com/@helen.walton.author